USA TODAY BESTSELLING AUTHOR

DALE MAYER

contemporary
romance

SCARS

BROKEN BUT... MENDING #2

SCARS
Beverly Dale Mayer
Valley Publishing Ltd.

Copyright © 2015

This is a work of fiction. Names, characters, places, brands, media, and incidents are either the product of the author's imagination or are used fictitiously. Any resemblance to actual events, locales, or persons, living or dead, is entirely coincidental.

ISBN-13: 978-1-988315-88-1
Print Edition

About This Book

Some scars are on the surface, others are in hiding, but the worst ones are buried so deep they refuse to be brought to the light…

Forced to deal with very deep and individual problems, Robin and Sean – strangers who are complete opposites – agree to an assisgnment that includes only the two of them and that initially seems radical and a little scary.

Separately, they've existed in private worlds, hiding in plain sight, not living and certainly not thriving. To move forward, they'll have to confront issues that have plagued them for most of their lives. Despite their differences, they discover they complement each other, and, in finding themselves, they also find each other…

Sign up to be notified of all Dale's releases here!

https://geni.us/DaleNews

CHAPTER 1

ROBIN CHILDERS WAITED at the side of the small conference room, her stomach in knots, her palms sweating. She did that a lot these days. Wait. Wait for the days to pass. Wait for the months to pass. Wait for time between her surgeries to pass.

To the next surgery she didn't want. Another surgery she had to have – or stay a freak that scared little children and caused horrified stares wherever she went.

Not the life she'd planned.

Not the life she'd imagined for herself.

Not the life she'd wanted.

But it was the life she was currently living. And that sucked.

Big time.

While watching the other participants enter, she had to acknowledge she wasn't alone in not liking her life.

Everyone appeared to be walking to death row. Here because of outside influences, because other people wanted them to attend. Or maybe here because they understood that they needed to be – yet hating the necessity that forced them to take this step. And yet they still came. Because they needed this.

Everyone was here for whatever magic their instructor psychologist / therapist, Professor Jenna Komak, had to offer.

In other words, they were all desperate.

To heal. To ditch the ugly in their lives. To find a way to live a 'normal' life – whatever that meant.

It was an odd thing to realize that she'd signed up for this on her own. Empowering. No one had pressured her to come. No one had paid the heavy fees for her. One brave morning, she'd determined that this was the next step in her journey, and she'd taken it.

She'd even managed to stay positive right up until it was time to leave for the workshop. Then reality hit her. Not only was she going to a seminar to help her deal with a painful issue, she was going to have to leave the university campus where she lived and travel to a hotel in downtown Vancouver. Be out in public. Deal with strangers.

At least at the university, people were used to seeing her. They stared, but less and less as they became accustomed to her face. Yet to do this workshop, she'd have to leave her hidey hole and journey out *there* – a place she'd hidden from as hard and as long as she could.

It had been easy to push the anxiety into a small hole in her stomach as she dreamed of the promise of finally getting the help she needed. That hope had kept her going. Now that she'd arrived, her gut in knots, her palms sweaty just from the thought of what she was doing. Doubts plagued her.

Damn. She was an idiot. A masochist. Maybe she needed her head examined after all. Something Jenna was sure to do. And that was pretty scary. Robin had issues. Duh.

Sure, everyone did. One of hers – the big one – she wore for the entire world to see. All other issues stemmed from there. Although if she were honest and more self-aware, she could probably find issues from her past at the root of this, too. But she had no plans to do that. She was here to deal with a specific issue. Not to try and deal with them all. There were too many. They hurt too much.

No. If she could deal with one issue, then she could return to a more normal life. The rest of her issues would have to wait until later. Much later.

It was her reaction – and other people's reactions to her face – that terrified her. And therein lay the problem.

She had to get over herself.

And that was a shitty deal.

Hating the inside shakiness threatening to take over the rest of her long frame, Robin turned to watch the other participants amble in to take their places. Her glance strayed past then caught on her friend Tania sitting silent at her side.

"Hey," Tania said, nervously.

She was just as nervous, maybe more so, but just as determined as Robin to move on in life. Only Tania's scars were inside. Hidden from the world. Private. She had the discretion to share on her time frame.

"Are you sure you're okay?" Robin asked her, studying her friend's face in concern.

Tania shrugged. "I'm fine."

Robin heard the tremor in Tania's voice, and then there was likely a matching one in hers.

The two of them were a mess.

Just then, Dr. Jenna Komak walked in.

And the class tension eased back. That woman exuded a presence. Calm. Capable. Caring.

She knew them all individually and they all knew her. Everyone here had attended evening classes with her and had been vetted and approved to take this special workshop.

Most of them were students from the same university. But not all. They were a mix of men and women.

Yet there was a common denominator – they were all damaged.

SEAN WILSON SLOUCHED in the back of the room. Separate from the others. Like he'd always been. He still questioned his sister's request. By rights, if he was here, Paris should be as well. And she'd wanted to come but had been refused, with a gentle suggestion to wait for another session a few months down the road. Maybe she'd be ready then.

Disappointed, Paris had then asked Sean to apply and if he got accepted, to scope it out for her. See if it would help her. He'd expected to be rejected even faster than Paris had been, so Sean had applied. And been accepted.

Paris had been overjoyed for him. Sean had been terrified. It was so not what he wanted. He didn't want to listen to other people's problems. He didn't want to share his own. He'd done a lot already. Was studying psychology to help him understand more. But that was on his time frame. Not here. Not now. Not surrounded by strangers. Who would want this? But there was no backing out now. He wouldn't be able to. Not and still face his sister.

Now he was here in the hotel, stuck, and likely to be spending a week in very uncomfortable situations trying to be polite in the group therapy sessions that rubbed him the wrong way. He'd been in those before. They were not fun.

He had no wish to have this prof dig around in his head. Regardless of the prof's cool confidence in her ability to help everyone.

He barely stifled back a snort at that thought. Looking

up, he realized several people were staring at him. So okay, he hadn't been as silent as he thought he'd been.

"What?" he asked the Goth-looking woman in front of him, giving her his bland face – willing her to say something.

The woman raised an eyebrow then smirked as if seeing something he hadn't expected her to see before turning away.

Damn right. He slouched back, stretched his long legs out in front of him and crossed his arms across his chest.

Sean had never backed down from a fight in his life. And had never apologized. He wasn't about to start now. Maybe he'd have saved himself a lot of pain if he'd learned that lesson as a child. Then again, he'd never been a fast learner. Besides, Paris was and it hadn't helped her any. She was the one that should be here. Damn. Why had Jenna thought Paris wasn't ready? And yet Jenna thought Sean was?

Although he hadn't come for help, or planned on being helped, there was room for it. His life was a mess of sleepless nights, bad nightmares during the few moments of shuteye he did get, followed by slow, dragging-his-ass days as he pulled himself through the daily requirements of being a human being on this planet.

Something he'd looked at cutting short a time or two. But not since becoming an adult.

And it was due to his sister that he hadn't completed the job. He might not be worth saving – but she was. She'd needed him to get *that* job done.

At least that's what he told himself. And none of it changed the fact that he was empty inside. Filled with pain and sorrow. He lived in the shadows. Alone. He looked normal to everyone else – calm as if he lived in the light.

Except there was no light in his soul. Just darkness.

And now he was in a seminar geared to drain some of that darkness away. But what if that darkness did disappear? And there was nothing left inside?

CHAPTER 2

G IVEN THAT LAST night had been the introduction to the workshop, along with an overview of what would take place this week in general terms, Robin knew today would be a case of getting down to business.

Especially now. The morning break was already over. Now there was a sense of waiting. Expectation. She glanced over at Tania to see her gaze locked on Jenna's face. They'd all hear about the special project Jenna had designed for each of them. That could go either way. Robin preferred to work alone. Although it would be fine to work with Tania, as she already understood Robin's issues and she was one of the few who understood some of Tania's.

Jenna had a stack of papers in front of her on a clipboard. Notes of some kind. Jenna didn't waste any time welcoming the group back. As if understanding that Jenna had shifted gears, several people sat straight up.

Robin slid lower in her seat.

"All right. We're going to start with the assignment that you will each do during the week."

She listened as Jenna outlined a weeklong project everyone would have to complete during their stay here. As she heard the general details, Robin couldn't help but feel a huge sense of relief inside. She lowered her gaze in case Jenna caught a glimpse of that look in her eyes. If Jenna saw, she'd change Robin's assignment. No one was allowed to be too comfortable – not in a workshop like this.

Still, she couldn't help but wonder what possible project she'd be called to do. School was easy for her, so a report didn't worry her. The project would also help her get through the week. Something to focus on so she could ignore the others. If she had to, she could even present it to this class. After all, here they were all equals. And all broken.

"I understand there could be some resistance to the individual assignments."

A ripple worked its way around the small seminar room.

A knowing smile slipped across Jenna's beautiful face. "Given that, I suggest you remember why you are here. What you hope to get out of this week, and keep in mind that you all came to me and in everyone's case..." she stopped to look each participant in the eye then continued, "I have evaluated your situation and came up with what I believe is the best way forward for each of you." She smiled, her gaze whispering back across their faces. "So remember that when you hear what I have planned."

Robin sat back and swallowed. Hard. Oh Lord. She wanted this to be a simple, school report type of project, but her gut said she wouldn't be so lucky.

And she wasn't.

"We'll start with Sean," Jenna said. "Please come to the back of the room with me and I can go over your assignment." Jenna looked down at the document in her hand and nodded once. She glanced up and pinned Robin in place. "Robin, you too. You'll be working with Sean."

Ah hell. So much for working with Tania. Or for working alone. She glanced over at Sean. She'd recognized the look in his eye earlier. He didn't want anything to do with this workshop. She had no idea why he was here, but it wasn't to heal. But from the look of him, he needed to do that very badly.

SURPRISED TO HEAR his name called first, Sean stood up and shoved his chair back out of the way. The beautiful professor motioned to the back of the room, presumably to discuss his project. Here went nothing.

Why was he here again? Still, it was just a project. He was already here, so what the hell. At least he'd be able to report back to Paris. He wondered what the project was. As he started weaving through the tables and chairs to the back of the room, he heard Jenna call out a second name as his partner. Partner? These were individual assignments – weren't they? Had he missed something? He hoped so. Teamwork was something he did well at school, at work. In his personal life – not so much. Sure, this was a category altogether – but there was no doubt this was damn personal. He was a loner. And that was by choice.

As Robin walked past him, he remembered her from last night, where she'd spent the better part of the 'getting to know everyone' session sitting in a corner and making it plain she had no intention of getting to know anyone. He understood that. He felt the same way but so far this morning, her attitude hadn't improved. If anything, from that slight curl of her lip, she'd taken a turn for the worse. She had stunning black hair that hung down straight over one side of her face so it appeared that she could only see half her world. Her hair was black and her skin cream, and it reminded him of a black and white personality.

Too bad for her.

Well, he could deal with whatever. This was only for a week. He'd tolerated much worse for much longer.

How hard could this be?

CHAPTER 3

NEEDING HER AIR of indifference to hide the inner turmoil, Robin sat down at the chair that Jenna indicated and crossed her legs. She waited. Sean sauntered over like he didn't give a damn. He probably didn't. With his attitude, Robin had no idea why he was here in the first place. He was odd. Tall and slim with wide shoulders and slim hips. He was built for gentlemen suits and wore jeans with more holes than material. It was that cocky "screw you" look on his face that she couldn't stop watching.

No one was that cynical naturally. Something bad had happened to him. It was the only reason for the aggressive front. And maybe he was afraid of it happening again. No, she studied the casual indifference as he flipped a long leg over the back of the chair to sit in the seat. No, it – whatever *it* was – would never happen to him again. That look on his face said he meant business. That curl of his lip – an almost dare you to try *it* again. That set of his shoulders almost waiting…he'd been hurt once, and he'd be damned if he'd allow that to happen again.

There'd be no repeats in Sean's life. No second chances. She doubted he knew what the word forgiveness meant. Yet he was here. At this workshop.

"Robin?"

Robin jerked, realizing that both Sean and Jenna were

staring at her as she'd stared blatantly at Sean. Color washed up her neck. Jenna's look was curious. Sean however, his look was purely aggressive. Shit. She straightened, plastered an apologetic smile on her face, and rushed to say, "I'm sorry. My mind was just caught on other things."

Out of the corner of her eye, she saw Sean's lips slide in a downward smirk. He didn't believe her. Knowing she'd be in for a very long week if they didn't get off on the right foot, she gave him a real smile and apologized sincerely.

His gaze narrowed in surprise.

She turned her gaze back onto Jenna's approving look and almost smiled again. Damn, she was going to turn into a real Girl Guide if she wasn't careful. Still, she hadn't meant to pry or be too inquisitive – not here. Everyone had secrets. And they were entitled to them.

Especially these people.

"It's fine. I don't mind if you look," he said mockingly.

The insinuation in his face had her back stiffening and her shoulders going straight. She turned to face him head on. "Good, then I'll look."

She returned his look with a mocking one of her own, her gaze sweeping him from head to foot. Then she gave him a tight smile, watching as one of his eyebrows shot straight up. So he wasn't used to people standing up for themselves. Especially women. Interesting. She filed that tidbit away.

"What do you see?" This time he seemed genuinely curious, not mocking.

She hesitated. She shouldn't tell him. He was an unknown quality to her. Violence lurked under the surface.

"Go ahead," he scoffed. "It's not like you know anything about me."

Still, Robin held back. She glanced over at Jenna to see

her watching the exchange, a tiny smile playing at the corner of Jenna's mouth. Damn. She wasn't going to step in and help.

Screw it. He'd asked, so he might as well know. "I see a man who's been so badly hurt he doesn't give a shit about anyone or anything – and especially not the world in general."

Silence.

He leaned forward and studied her face, what he could see of it. She glared at him defiantly.

"I thought the head doctor sat in the other chair." He snorted. "What are you, some kind of amateur hobbyist? You like to dig into people and see what makes them tick?"

"I like to watch people," she said, holding the defensive note tight inside. "And there are a lot of people out there to watch."

"Then watch *them*. Not me." After delivering that short terse message, he sat back and stared at Jenna.

At least the attitude was gone. She turned to face Jenna. "So what is the assignment?"

Jenna rifled through her papers but as far as Robin could see, it was more a ruse to give the two of them time to calm down. As if. Robin waited impatiently for Jenna to reorganize the papers then pick up the top one.

"A friend of mine coordinates special programs," Jenna said, peering over her paper at Robin as she added, "at a local hospital."

Robin stiffened. Nothing like bringing up hospitals to push her buttons. Then Jenna would know that. Forcing herself to relax, she tried to stem the panic that was churning in her gut. If just the word hospital could do that to her...

"BC Children's Hospital," Jenna said.

Robin gasped. No, not a children's hospital. Robin stared at Jenna in shock. She didn't understand why her feet hadn't already taken her the hell away from this room and from this woman. She didn't dare plead with Jenna for a new project but damn it, she wanted to.

She couldn't do children.

Not today. Not tomorrow. Never.

"Andrea has agreed to have you and Sean spend some time there so you can complete this report."

Robin went numb inside. Everything shut down. She couldn't hear Jenna's words. She wouldn't hear them. But the response tumbled from her lips. "You do understand that you are subjecting these children to a horrific sight – right?"

Jenna smiled. "Am I?

She didn't dare look at Sean to gauge his reaction. Then again, he'd likely have no problem with this part.

It didn't matter. She couldn't do it. She couldn't do hospitals. She couldn't do children.

Shuddering, she stood up and stumbled against her chair. She half-registered that Sean had leapt to his feet to help her but she managed to avoid him. *Leave. Get away.* That was all she could think about. She had to escape.

She reeled backwards, then seeing a space between the chair and the wall, she took it, bolting for her freedom. For a world that didn't involve projects, hospitals...or children.

SEAN TURNED BACK to look at Jenna. "Well, aren't you going to go after her?"

Jenna smiled in that calm, serene way of hers. "No, I'll wait for her to come back."

"Come back?" He twisted around to look at the way

Robin had raced out then turned back to glare at Jenna. "Why the hell would she?"

"Because it's what she wants." She lowered her head to read the documents in front of her.

Frustrated, Sean didn't know what to do. He glanced around at the others but outside of the casual glance his way, no one appeared to have noticed Robin's outburst.

"Why don't I do the project on my own? You can come up with a different one for her." Hell, he could do that easily. He didn't necessarily like children, but he didn't hate them. Not wanting to do something was not the same as being incapable.

All of a sudden he realized he was standing awkwardly in front of Jenna, trying to figure out what just happened. While he could empathize with Robin for Jenna pushing her buttons, she knew there'd be lots of that happening this week. She should have been prepared for it.

If anyone could prepare for sudden silent sabotage of one's deepest fears…

Then again, he had to trust in Jenna. She'd had incredible results with her program. If she could help Robin – good. He didn't trust anyone – particularly when it came to his head or heart.

And as long as Jenna stayed out of his head, she could do what she needed to do to help Robin. Because Robin obviously needed her. Although he'd suggest using something a lot less violent than the two-by-four Jenna had already hit her with.

The noise level in the room continued and somehow…the other participants managed to ignore what was happening in this corner…or were doing a good imitation of it. Likely it was a case of self-preservation as they'd be here themselves soon. He glanced around and caught a couple of people looking up, only to drop their gaze when he caught them staring at him, but he got that reaction a lot from people.

He stared down at his feet and considered his own actions. It seemed he'd acted out of character himself. He'd jumped to his feet to help Robin when he'd seen her distress, his hand out to her. He'd instinctively tried to go after her. Even now, he could barely stifle the urge.

And how did that work? Normally he wouldn't have given a shit. He didn't get involved in people's lives. He hated drama. Except in the case of his sister.

For her, he'd do anything.

But Robin wasn't his sister. She didn't look or sound or act like her. So why the hell had he reacted? Or was it because Robin hurt like Paris hurt?

"Sean? Why don't you sit down?"

He turned back to stare at his empty chair and then at Jenna. He really was standing there like a dolt in the middle of the room. He relaxed his hand, realizing for the first time that he'd been standing with clenched fists.

Shit.

Catching her concerned glance, he said, "I'm fine." And threw himself into the chair to wait. If Jenna could sit there calmly, then so could he. He slumped lower in his chair, leaned his head back and closed his eyes.

This place was making him crazy already.

"I'm sorry."

Robin's soft voice hit him hard, the hurt in her tone making his stomach cramp. Her simple apology hit him harder. She said it easily, the words flowing off her lips. He had so little practice he doubted he could have done so well in these awkward circumstances.

He opened his eyes and rolled his head sideways to see Robin standing in front of him and Jenna – much as he had a moment ago with her hands clenched into fists. He stared at the long fingers, seeing the white-knuckled grip, and saw his sister in her yet again. That was so Paris. Take a hit, run away long enough to collect herself, then come back and face the music – or more often than not – take another hit. It both pissed him off and made him admire her. Something he didn't want. He didn't want to feel anything for anyone. Especially not others as screwed up as these people were.

Damn, he needed a shrink. And groaned. Look where the hell he was. He turned to watch Jenna.

Jenna smiled up at her gently. "That's fine. I'm glad you're feeling better. I only need another moment to finish the instructions."

Robin sat down on the edge of her chair and listened quietly.

He gave Robin full points for demeanor. She appeared locked down but was holding on. He couldn't have been so calm. A few moments later, he wasn't calm at all.

Shocked, he listened to the rest of Jenna's final instructions. "What are you talking about? I'm not going to sketch these kids."

Hearing a strangled sound from beside him, he glanced over at Robin, remembering her earlier words to Jenna. Why would the kids be scared? What the hell was going on here? He hated knowing there were undercurrents he didn't understand. He was only here for his sister's sake. Hell, she was the one that should be here. Paris loved kids. She'd do fine with this project.

Him not so much. Good thing he didn't give a damn.

As his glance slid across Robin's face, he thought he caught a glimpse of something, but he'd just missed it. His eyes drifted past then hit reverse.

And locked on Robin's face. Was that a tear? Not that he could see much of her with hair covering most of her face. What the hell was going on here? His gaze switched from Jenna's, which was full of compassion, to Robin's, whose head was down as she stared at her feet. Her lower lip trembled, too.

Ah shit.

There were a lot of things in life he could handle and there were a lot he couldn't. A lady's tears topped that last list.

"Sean, you don't have to," Jenna paused before adding smoothly, "In fact, I want you to sketch Robin with the kids."

Robin groaned softly as if in pain.

Hating this, Sean glared at the woman who had the ability to get under his skin like no other. She saw things… private, personal things… "How did you even know that I draw?"

Jenna's lips slowly tilted into a full-blown smile that made his stomach roll. What was she up to? "You were doodling in the evening lectures – something to keep you occupied while your sister attended," she added the last bit with wry humor. "And those doodles were good. Not only that, but you are a seriously gifted artist."

"Really?" He threw up his hands. "So what if I doodle? That's it. I don't do portraits." After a moment, he added, "And I certainly don't do pretty."

Now her smile deepened with understanding and empathy. He couldn't look. He shifted his gaze in Robin's direction. Her eyes were downcast, her hands clasped on her knees as if not even hearing the conversation.

Sean waited in uncomfortable silence. Damn it. "Look," he said, exasperated and starting to feel cornered, a situation guaranteed to get his back up. He hated being forced into doing anything. "Just give us the assignment and we'll take it from there."

This time, Jenna laughed. "You already have it."

He stared at her, his mind trying to grasp what it was obviously missing. "What? Just draw pictures of Robin and the kids? That's it."

"No, that's not it. You need to find a theme that fits Robin. I want you to study her and see the theme that runs through everything she does. Everything she is. And that's what you draw. Not Robin and the kids. The theme of Robin."

She stood up, and Sean realized he wasn't going to be able to ask much more. "Wait," he said, "Why did you pair me up with Robin?"

And Jenna's smile brightened. "Thank you for asking that," she said. "As part of your assignment, at the very end, you will answer that question for me."

"Ah hell," he muttered. Served him right for opening his mouth. He should have known better. After all, his mouth had gotten him into a lot of trouble as a child.

But like any other stubborn, knot-headed male, he'd grown more defiant, angrier, and the cycle had just repeated.

Robin didn't seem to be too affected by the conversation. She still seemed completely frozen in place.

"I'll leave you to think about this for a few moments while I go and discuss another group's projects with them." And she stood up and walked back to the rest of the participants, calling out two other people's names. When Sean turned back to Robin, it was to find her walking out the door to the main lobby. Alone.

CHAPTER 4

ROBIN WALKED INTO the dining room and took a seat in the corner at the far end, her back to the wall. The one place where she felt safe. From here, she could watch everyone else. Damn, there was Sean. She didn't want to have lunch with him. In fact, she wanted as little to do with him as possible. He disturbed her on so many levels.

Not only because he'd seen her little emotional breakdown, but because of his sudden jump to help and his standing between her and Jenna. He might not realize how that looked, but Robin knew. Jenna would also know exactly what it meant. She doubted Sean had any idea there was a white knight lurking inside that cold, derisive exterior.

He might have his mile-high defenses between him and the real world, but it appeared to be a little thin when he came in contact with girls in trouble.

Sean walked over and sat down across from her.

Because he was okay to leave his back exposed to the others and had just enough self-confidence to not give a damn, irritation flared.

"There are other places to sit," she muttered, not capable of being abrasive and cold.

"There are. But as we need to discuss some of the issues about this project," he motioned for the waitress to come over before turning back to her. "I figured this would be a good time to get a few things settled."

She stared at him. "Like what?

"Bus or car?"

"Bus."

Instant and honest. She hated travelling in cars. Not since her accident. She took the bus everywhere.

"Okay, maybe I should have said truck or bus."

She stopped and frowned at him. "Truck?"

"I have a heavy duty Dodge Ram."

She watched the water droplet on the side of her water glass slide down the side. She touched it with her fingertip and ran the wetness across the glass. She sighed. "Still a bus."

"Fine. But you might want to consider that it will mean being in each other's company for longer, and it'll be harder to get to the hospital on a daily basis."

She stiffened and turned her gaze to look outside the window. "Why the hospital?" she murmured.

"I wasn't exactly thrilled to be going there myself, but as it's Jenna's project and we came here trusting in her…"

Robin shot him a scornful look. "Like you give a shit. Why are you here anyway? It's not like you want to be helped. And if you're not doing this for yourself, why are you here?" Her mind spun on the possibilities. She couldn't help testing a couple of them. "Unless you're being forced to attend? Or attending to help someone else?"

He stared at her. "Why the hell would I sit through this garbage and do this stupid report for someone else?"

There wasn't much redeeming about that tone of voice, but there was something…something in his eyes that said she was on the right track. "Because you want to help someone. You're a fraud, you know?"

He leaned forward, his fists clenched. "If you were a

man, I'd…"

She leaned forward, glaring at him nose to nose and said, "What? Punch me out? Is that how you solve everything? Physical violence?"

An odd look came over his face. He took a shaky breath and sat back. He stared out the window at the people walking by. Just then, the waitress came and asked for their order. Robin ordered a cheeseburger and a salad. Sean, without even looking at the menu, ordered a burger and fries.

"That's what I mean. You want to wreak violence, but only a small part of you does. I have no doubt," she rushed to say at the glint coming into his eyes, "that given an opportunity to beat down on someone, you'd dive right in. But they'd have to deserve it."

And damn if he didn't stare back at her like she'd just lost her head. "What the hell are you talking about?" He shook his head. "You know nothing about me."

She smiled. "I know more than you think."

SHE BETTER NOT. Brooding, he sat across from one of the biggest mixed-up females he'd met in a long time. Of course he'd also seen more of her than he had anyone else in a long time. She'd had a breakdown at the thought of the children's hospital, ran away, came back, then chose a seat at the furthest corner in the restaurant to watch everyone like a hawk. She might be studying him, and damn, she seemed to be doing a good job of understanding him too, but she didn't *know* him.

If she really knew him, she'd have run screaming out the door already.

Like everyone else had.

He wasn't the most popular guy. That was okay. He had his sister. Paris was softer, gentler than he was. She'd taken the path of least resistance and had suffered more for it then. He'd taken the full frontal aggressive route, but he was suffering more now.

At least that's what Paris said he was doing. He thought it was all psychobabble. Still, he loved her. She loved him. They had each other, and there'd never been anyone else in their lives for more than a night or two. Neither had a partner in any real sense of the word – only each other. Through the tough times, that had been enough.

Except Paris wanted more in her life. Children. A husband. To be loved in every sense of the word. Sean wasn't sure that she could ever have such a thing. And he knew he couldn't. So it was not something he'd ever brought into his psyche as a wish or a want. Why yearn for what he couldn't have? But Paris did, and by God, he'd do what he could to see her get it.

One of them deserved to know what happiness was.

"What is it?"

The voice penetrated the black cloud in his mind. He started, realizing he'd been glaring out the window. With considerable effort, he pulled himself out of the place he always ended up in – regardless of his best efforts to not go there.

Moodily, he played with the fork on the table. Pivoting it over end to end. He didn't know what to say.

"Never mind. It's obvious that the subject is painful."

He raised his gaze to stare at her, marveling that her hairstyle completely hid the one half of her face. Why? Was she blind in that one eye to the extent that it didn't bother

her to only see with half her normal vision?

"It's not painful," he said abruptly. Then frowned. Why the hell had he said that?

"Well, it can't be pleasant. You looked like you wanted to kill someone."

He smiled darkly, remembering his thoughts. "Can't. That's already been done."

She raised her eyebrows and narrowed her gaze at him.

Let her think he was a killer. Let her think the worst of him. That would keep her away.

"Well, if that's the case, you didn't kill them."

Damn. Was she for real? "Who are you, Pollyanna?"

It was her turn to frown. "I don't know the reference."

He waved his hand. "Really? Loosely, it means you have a positive-look-only-on-the-bright-side-of-life attitude."

"I don't," she protested. "I'm nothing like that."

"So you decided I haven't killed anyone? Are you nuts? I'm perfectly capable of killing."

"Oh, absolutely." She grinned. "But only in the right circumstances."

He stopped in the act of picking up his coffee cup, stared, then shook his head. "You aren't making any sense." Trust him to get paired with a lightweight in the brain department.

"You are capable, but you haven't done it yet. That's probably part of the anger. You wanted to be able to do something like that, but you couldn't..."

Just as he was about to lash out at her again, she added, "...someone beat you to it."

Holy crap. She was dangerous. How the hell had she figured that out? And what was he going to do about it?

Just as he was about to open his mouth and Lord only

knew what was about to pour forth – because he had no idea – the waitress arrived and placed full steaming plates down. He had a massive amount of fries in front of him. On cue, his stomach grumbled. The waitress was rattling off something about enjoying their meal, but he was already reaching for one long particularly good-looking fry on his plate – when it was snatched out from under him.

Astonished, he could only follow its trail where it disappeared into Robin's mouth.

She caught his look and grinned. Then she laughed and laughed.

When she could, she said, "Sorry, that fry had my name on it." She giggled again. "And the look on your face was so worth it."

Stunned, but at her huge face-splitting smile that completely transformed her features, he picked up another fry and studied her. When she'd laughed, her hair had moved slightly. Now that she was eating, the hair was brushed out of her way with a quick movement of her hand. And he realized that the hair was more than a style. It was a front. Behind which hid scars. And from what he could see, they were long and ugly.

Hence the comment about what Jenna might be subjecting the children to.

He ate slowly, thinking about all the things her and Jenna had said…and not said, and realized that this was likely one of the core issues why Robin was here. The one side of her face was stunning with pure white skin and huge green eyes that could cloud with emotion or twinkle with laughter. Her hairstyle was dramatic and eye-catching. But she kept to herself and avoided letting anyone see the other side of her face. And now he understood why.

What impact it was going to have, he didn't know. But as they had a lot of work to get done, maybe honesty was the best policy.

Deciding to be upfront, he asked, "What happened to your face? House fire or car accident?"

She stilled, then choked on her food. She swallowed hard, her gaze flickering in his direction then back at her burger. He kept his gaze steady, figuring he already knew the answer.

Finally, she reached for the glass of water and took a long drink. Her voice was cool and controlled as she said, "Why?"

"Considering what we have ahead of us, I'd appreciate knowing how your face became scarred."

She stared at him, belligerent but direct. God, he loved that about her. She never seemed to back down. Maybe it would get irritating if she turned out to be one of those women who needed to pick fights to clear the air or one who just liked to cause trouble – create a little drama. Yet it was refreshing to see someone with enough backbone to stand up to him.

"I'll tell you if you tell me how you got your scars."

Ouch. He hadn't seen that one coming. He settled back slightly. "What scars?"

She used her fork to point at the open collar of his shirt, then moved it to the side of his neck by his ear before it finally dropped to his hand. Scarred areas visible to the eye of anyone looking. He'd given up trying to hide the scars a long time ago. They were small and not unsightly. The biggest scars were inside. Of course it was a different story once he took his shirt off. But that rarely happened in daylight and as he wasn't physically self-conscious – who gave a damn?

But she was right. They both had scars. If he wanted answers, then she had the right to ask for answers as well. His usual lie well-prepared, he opened his mouth and out came the truth instead. "I was abused as a child."

His own gaze widened in shock as the truth came out. A truth he never shared. Jenna knew. Paris knew of course. She'd been there. But that was it. Except for the odd doctor and social worker or case worker. People without faces. Where he was a number only. A statistic to help fill in the dots on their data graphs.

Her eyes widened first in shock then softened in sympathy.

That part he didn't like. He said brusquely, "Your turn."

"It was a car accident." She winced. "My father was driving my mother, brother, and me to a special event. I'm the only one that survived."

And damn if she didn't chip away at another stone on the defensive wall he'd built to keep others out. A wall he'd never been in danger of having any breach before.

But this woman…she had weapons he had no defenses against.

One of them was her forthright honesty.

CHAPTER 5

ROBIN PLOWED THROUGH her cheeseburger, her mind screaming with things she wanted to say. Only her mouth was focused on getting the food down. She had wondered when she'd seen the small scars. If he'd been abused like he said, chances were there were many more scars under his clothing. Ones he could hide. She couldn't.

She wished they didn't have to go to the children's hospital. Her stomach twisted at the thought. Not to mention she had to get there somehow first.

Given the scale of her accident, she rarely shared the details. There was no point. It was hard enough to deal with people's reaction to her face – and the rest of her body, but if they knew the rest – yeah, that was more than she could handle. At least most of the people in the hospital either knew already or didn't bother asking many questions. They'd seen and heard it all before. She had no idea how they could handle all the sad cases day in and day out, but they did, and for that she was grateful. They'd made her time in the hospital that much easier. Not easy, mind you. There was nothing easy about this process.

"Are you having reconstructive surgery done?

A simple and calm question.

She responded in kind. "I've had many. There are many more to go." She shrugged. Might as well tell him the truth.

"I've had enough. Of always being in the hospital. Of trying to deal with the pain and the drugs. Of slowly recovering. The cycle just never ends."

He nodded. "So you've put them on the back burner for now."

"It sounds simple, doesn't it?" She quirked her lips, staring down at her plate, not seeing the half-demolished food. "But it's not. No one understood when I said enough."

"No one else is going through what you are going through, so how could they? At the most, people can empathize – they can't understand unless they've been there."

God, he was scary. He understood. And by his own words, he'd been there. She assessed the small scars and then studied the broad shoulders. He'd likely had a few surgeries himself.

"The shrink stuff is hard, too," she muttered.

"Actually," his voice deepened, "I think the shrinks are the worst." His gaze wandered over her face, studying the side she carefully kept hidden from the world. "I could deal with the physical pain as I healed, but the emotional pain, the healing of the mind – now that part was torture."

And he went back to eating his fries.

She understood so much of what he'd just said and yet he said it so casually. He'd admitted so much freely. It made her question her assumptions about him. She didn't think he'd open up easily, yet he'd admitted so much so fast.

Maybe they had more in common that she'd first thought.

Her cell phone dinged. She checked the incoming text then winced. "Jenna says the person we're to meet is available after 1pm today."

Sean, his own phone in his hand, said, "Good."

She glanced over at him in surprise. "What's good about it?"

"The faster we do this, the faster it's over."

She couldn't argue with that.

"Back to the earlier question – my truck or the bus? I understand why the bus given your history, but the truck would be more private and faster. We'd be there in less than fifteen minutes."

He waited, seemingly unconcerned about her answer. She wanted to take the damn bus. "Truck."

And found satisfaction in the flicker of surprise in his eyes. He didn't know her as well as he thought. Then again, as she stared at her hand starting to shake with nerves, maybe she didn't know herself either.

HE WONDERED WHAT her impulse would cost her. Would she actually get in his truck? He knew driving was riskier, but in his truck, she was as safe as anything other than fate could keep her. It wasn't new but it was big and solid.

He paid the lunch bill, aware that she hadn't even noticed, now all balled up inside at the idea of sitting in a vehicle again. Then again, this is what these types of sessions were all about. He could help her do this.

He was good at helping out. It kept the focus off him.

Grasping her arm above the elbow, he led her out to the vehicle, not giving her time to back out. If he let her go to her hotel room and change or even collect something to bring with them, she'd changed her mind. Better to drag her forward and have her face this.

She moved like a robot beside him. Perfect.

He clicked the remote lock and unlocked the passenger door. He led her straight there, opened the truck door, and half-lifted her in. Without wasting any movement, he reached across and snapped her seatbelt in place and snugged it up tight. Then he shut the door and walked around to his side.

She never said a word.

Neither did she move a muscle.

He hopped in, buckled up, and started up the engine. To ease the silence, he turned on the radio, then after a careful look around, he pulled the truck out of the hotel parking lot. A good driver already, he drove extra careful today.

Once he was back out on the main street, which was a short straight run up to the hospital, he glanced over at her. That she was still sitting and hadn't tried to bolt said a lot about where she was at in life right now. His gaze landed on her white-knuckled grip on the seatbelt strap. Or not.

"You're doing great. We're almost there."

She made a small, almost indiscernible sound.

"Another couple of minutes more," he said quietly. Sure enough, he could almost see the huge building from the road. He pulled ahead and made the turn to bring him into the back lot of the hospital. He heard Robin let out a heavy raspy breath.

"How did you know where to go?" she asked her, her voice subdued.

"I've lived in Vancouver all my life." He winced. "And it's the only children's hospital here."

There was a long silence as she digested his words. "I'm sorry."

"Don't be. You didn't do it, and it was a long time ago."

"It might have been a long time ago, but that doesn't mean I have to like the cruelty."

He pulled into a parking space and turned off the engine. It was only as he opened his door to exit that he realized that she was referring to his childhood. "I…" he said, slamming the truck door and coming around to help her out, "don't either."

Together, a truce of some kind settling inside, they walked into the building he'd spent way too much time in as a child and a young teen. If he wasn't receiving care, Paris was. She'd suffered so much more than he had. He'd been hurt, but she'd been victimized in the worst of ways over and over again. He'd been unable to stop it and when he had finally had the chance, like Robin had guessed, someone else had done the job for him.

Maybe that was a good thing. He didn't think once he'd started stabbing the bastard that he'd have been able to quit until the old man was nothing but hunks of raw meat.

He had to wonder what his life would have been like if the rage that had consumed him that day hadn't spent itself. There'd been one cop whom he'd swung at, the bloodthirst and rage still burning bright, who'd let him hit it out, kick and punch and fight until he couldn't fight any more, and the cop never once laid a hand on him in retaliation. Only as a way to restrain him so he didn't get hurt himself. When he'd finally crumpled to the ground, a mess of bleeding raw emotion, the cop had said that he now needed to help his sister.

From that moment on, he'd been there for her like he hadn't been able to be there for her before.

He thought of that cop a lot but hadn't seen the man since. What did it take to be someone who could see the need in a child to pound someone to the ground and take the blows while not hitting back? To come from a place of such deep understanding that he allowed himself to be the target for as long as that child had needed? Did that cop know he'd saved Sean's soul that day, even as Paris had saved his life earlier?

Since that day, Sean had never had the anger return to the same extent. Whenever it did rise up now, it was lighter, softer, and less intense. He knew that one day that rage would no longer be there. He could see that now. The cop must have seen it then.

For that, Sean would always be grateful.

He glanced over at Robin and wondered how she'd vented.

Had she vented?

Or was she, like Paris, walking around, the raw wound open and still oozing day in and day out without ever having a way to heal?

He couldn't think of anything worse.

At least he'd managed to punch and kick out at the world at the damage that had been inflicted on him and his beloved sister. His hard-won healing had started from that point forward.

CHAPTER 6

THE TRUCK RIDE was over. She'd actually ridden in a vehicle again – and survived. She wanted to laugh and jump and cry all at the same time. Only she was afraid it would end in tears – hysterical ones at that. It was stupid to feel so overwhelmed. She'd call the venture a success but as it would not have happened without Sean putting her in, buckling her up, and locking her down to keep her there, it was hardly *her* success. She'd been white-knuckled the whole time. She glanced down at the nail indents in the palm of her hands. At least she hadn't cut the skin.

The sun shone high above, a bright beautiful sky signaling that she was alive and life was good. Privately, she admitted, now that the trip was over, it hadn't been that bad.

Now if she could get through the next hour or so.

As if afraid that she'd bolt, Sean hooked her arm into his and led the way through the imposing double-door entrance of the huge building ahead of them.

Inside the hospital, Robin tugged back on Sean's arm to stop and look around. And take some deep breaths. Just the noise, the smell…memories hurtled back into her mind, bringing back the same panic she'd experienced before her last surgery. And memories from even before that. Tears collected at the corner of her eyes.

She couldn't do this.

She didn't want to do this.

She *had* to do this. Oh God. She closed her eyes and worked on regaining her sense of balance. It was either that or take off back to Sean's truck. She shuddered. And then what? Get back in the vehicle and wait for him to do his thing here?

So scared she could hardly move, a sound slowly penetrated. Off to the left, someone wept quietly. Low deep sobs. Female sobs. Sobs that seared into Robin's heart. She'd heard enough of those. From patients she couldn't help. From the families of those she couldn't help. From herself.

Hospitals seemed to thrive on pain. Sure, many patients walked out in better shape than they walked in, but so many never walked out. These places were both lifesavers and the worst kind of hell for some. She wasn't sure which side of that divide she stood on right now. She hadn't been able to handle it the last few times she'd been in one.

Sean tugged on her hand, bringing her attention back to her surroundings. She glanced over at him, seeing the concerned frown on his face. She shrugged, struggling for control, and said, "I'm fine."

"You don't look it."

"I just want to look around." She didn't dare tell him that this was hard for her. Hell, it wasn't like he didn't get it. She'd been standing there like an idiot for the last five minutes. Obviously something was wrong with her. Did Sean understand what she'd gone through in a different hospital? Alone?

Even if he did, he didn't know about her connection to *this* hospital. She'd sworn to never go back into a hospital for all the reasons she was experiencing right now. The panic. The inability to breathe. She might have panic attacks in her life now, but she swore they'd started while she'd been in the hospital.

She was a mess, and a lot of that was triggered by being in here.

At another hard tug on her hand, she squared her shoulders obstinately, needing another moment to try and see her surroundings rationally.

The reception was oriented to younger children, with the sitting area decorated with bright animal pictures painted on the wall. The large waiting area was mostly a playroom for the younger kids. There was so much here, but was geared to the kids and not the parents whose lives were torn by the events that brought them here.

Sean tugged at her again, nudging her toward the elevators on the left side. With a last glance at the full playroom, she followed him. Tough day already for her. She'd taken a trip inside a truck and was even now standing inside a hospital. Hard to believe.

But she'd managed so far. Now to get through the next hour…then do it all over again in reverse. She was afraid she'd lose her lunch as her stomach started to heave. Instead, her gut locked down. Her chest squeezed tight. She couldn't breathe.

"Are you okay?" Sean gave her arm a slight shake.

After swallowing hard, she shot him a look as her world stabilized. She was here with him, for a report. Not for a trip down memory lane. Thankfully, she had something to focus on. She gave herself a shake and straightened her shoulders. "I'm fine."

"You should be," he said in a serious tone. "You've already beat back several demons."

That surprised her. She shrugged dismissively. "Doesn't

feel like I came out the winner."

"That's because the day isn't over." And he grinned.

The kindness and light in that grin shocked her. Warmed her. It almost felt like a hug.

Just then, the elevator doors opened and she was saved from having to answer. They stepped out. Sean automatically turned right and she followed. She had the name of the person that Jenna had said would be waiting for them but didn't have a clue where to find this person.

Sean appeared to. He walked through a series of doors and led her into a different world. As if he understood where these doors were actually going to take them. A world he recognized.

One of chaos. One of noise. One of children.

As if a whistle had been blown, the children realized they had company.

Silence fell. The kids stared at Sean, and then shifted to Robin.

She gasped. Her insides locked down and fear pulsed through her. *She could not do this.* She dropped her gaze to the floor, grateful her hair covered her face.

And she shut down.

IN AN INSTANT, silence switched to chaos.

Sean stared at the craziness going on in the large room. After giving him and Robin both a long assessing look, the kids returned to doing what they'd been doing originally. Playing. There were multiple couches, tables and even a couple of beds on both sides of the room. At this end, some children were lying quietly watching the others. In the middle and at the far end, there was chaos as children played video games and....

Some kind of party must be going on. He didn't remember any laughter or screaming for joy when he'd been here as a patient. And he'd been here lots. Not long enough to get to know anyone. But often enough for the staff to get to know him. Then again, he'd never been in a common room like this one.

He couldn't help that shrinking sensation with his emotions before they rolled free in a totally inappropriate way. At least, inappropriate for here. He couldn't rant and rave over the things done in the past anymore. He'd dealt with it all as much as he could – at the time and ever since. But every once in a while something – someone – got to him.

Like this group of kids. When this was over, he was going to hit the bar tonight. Not that he could drink himself into oblivion. He never did. That required a level of trust of the fellow man that he didn't have. But a few to take the edge off – maybe. No. Definitely.

"Hello?" A tall woman in a nurse's matched set strode toward them, a spring to her step and a bounce to her ponytail. Her smile – it was breathtaking.

Sean took a deep breath and raised his voice slightly to be heard over the din. "Hello. We're looking for Andrea Schulenburg."

"And you found her." The woman tapped her name tag, bringing Sean's attention to the name and position she held but before he could read it, she'd already turned and called back to two kids who appeared to be trying to have a sword fight with plastic knives.

A grin tugged at his mouth. He did love the resilience of kids. He had no idea why any of them were here but there were kids in bandages, wheelchairs, and casts. Some appeared to be missing limbs and still recovering from surgery, and still others were prone and hooked up to multiple tubes. Some of those kids lay unaffected; others smiled wistfully at the other kid's antics. The nurse called out. "Mark and Brian, no bouncing on the beds, please."

The boys jumped up and landed on their butts one final time before putting the plastic knives away. Interesting that she'd complained about the jumping but not the swordplay. While he'd been a patient here, he didn't remember being allowed either. Then again, it probably depended on the group of kids that were patients at any one time, group dynamics being what they were.

"I presume you are Sean Wilson and Robin Childers."

Sean nodded, seeing Robin not acknowledging the question in any way, her head down. Her fists clenched and released in a pattern he knew all too well. He tried to cover for her, saying pleasantly, "Yes. Thanks so much for letting us come."

"The kids are happy to have some excitement to brighten up their day." She smiled up at them. "Sean, I understand you are doing an artistic study. Do you have some kind of plan for what you want to happen here? A theme that I can help organize the children for?"

Sean looked at Robin sideways, a little lost on that theme aspect. If she had anything to contribute? She'd gone so still.

As in frozen.

Crap. His protective instincts rose to the surface and he shifted slightly, deliberately placing himself in front of Robin. He wished he could do this report alone. Robin might *need* to do it, but he wasn't seeing any sign that she was *ready* to.

Andrea stared at him, waiting. Right, she'd asked something about the theme. Sean didn't know what to say. Hell, he had no idea himself. He shrugged. "I don't have a theme in mind yet. I'll be doing some sketches of the kids. So I just need a place to sit and work."

And a place for Robin to hide. She'd be of no use today. Not that he had any idea what she was supposed to do here anyway. It would have been good to know her issues with children were so traumatic. He had some issues too, but more than that, he wanted to keep his inner child at a distance. That child caused a ruckus when he was free.

Staying detached from these kids would be harder. If he could focus on the artwork, he could avoid getting hooked on the kids. He hoped.

"Just a table? Do you need the kids quiet?" she asked, doubt coloring her voice even as her eyes darted from one child to another.

"Ha." He laughed, gesturing at the room behind her. "That doesn't look possible."

A bright grin transformed her face again. "No, at least not for long."

"Motion," Sean said. "They are all in motion. That could make my job difficult."

Andrea laughed. "They are kids. As soon as they heal enough to be able to move, they are constantly in motion." Her smile slipped. "Many are in between treatments. This is an escape for them. A release. Until the next time. And it's just as important as their surgeries."

"Sleep hard and play hard." Sean watched the kids shift to yet another game. In a way, he was glad he'd seen this. He was here now as an adult. He could look back on the memories and keep them in their rightful place. This scene completely eclipsed his memories of the pain…and the shame. And that was a good thing. The sketches were going to be fun and lively. Just like the subjects.

Trying to pull himself out of the weird mood that had suddenly set in and yes, to compensate for Robin's odd behavior, he turned to look around and saw a small table off the side by the window. A couple of chairs were there on the opposite side. He pointed to it. "How about over there?"

"Actually, I was just about to ask if that would work." Andrea was already walking over and moving chairs about so there were two on one side and one on the other. "This should give you a decent amount of light, and you can see the kids from here."

Grabbing Robin's arm, he led her over. Once there, Sean dropped his bag on the table. It made a louder thunk than he was expecting.

Robin jumped. She stared from the bag to him and back at the bag as if just now seeing it for the first time. He frowned. What the hell? She was acting really out of it. And it didn't look like she'd be pulling herself together anytime soon. He was afraid she'd explode, she was wound up so tight.

In a sudden move, she grabbed a chair, pulled it back, and sat down. He watched her as she watched the kids surreptitiously. She was acting both fascinated and re-pelled…yet…there was a hint of loneliness, sadness. He turned to watch the same two boys who'd been sword playing and were now arguing, and he could almost under-stand.

He didn't have any good memories of childhood, but he understood what had been the best thing – Paris. Having his twin there meant he'd never been alone. They'd fought and played from instant to instant. In all things, the one lesson he'd learned as a child was to enjoy the moment. It was always over too soon.

CHAPTER 7

THE SMELL…

Robin kept a smile pinned to her face. The children wouldn't notice if it was real or not. They'd be too busy studying every aspect of her and making a decision based on nebulous things like instinct. Hopefully they'd ignore her. She needed them to. As she needed to ignore them. It was the only way she could survive the next hour. Just the sound of their play made the bile rise up the back of her throat. They'd see her any moment now. Damn. She'd turned her back on them, but they were kids.

They'd come closer any second now.

She swallowed hard, her mind racing for things she could say when they came. She didn't want to be mean to any of them – they were obviously going through stuff of their own, but no one here seemed to understand how much more trauma they'd go through if they saw her face.

She'd seen it firsthand. She knew how the kids would react. The adults had a hard time with her too… but it was the children she was trying to save. Damn Jenna. How could she do this to them? They were sweet, innocent little kids. They didn't need more monster faces to wake them up in the middle of the night. No child deserved that.

Lost inside, she was oblivious to what Sean was doing. A shudder slipped down her spine. What if she just left? She could sit out in the main lobby and wait. Though that wouldn't be fair to Sean. Except that she'd have to deal with kids there, too. Maybe if she could keep her face hidden and stay silent, they wouldn't realize she was here.

It would be best for everyone.

Andrea had disappeared somewhere – likely back to the far end where the kids were. Good. One less person here to make her feel uncomfortable. Immediately she kicked herself. God, how selfish. This wasn't about her. She was trying to save them.

"Robin?"

She glanced up enough to see Sean out of her one eye. He was frowning at her. Of course he was. She wasn't exactly contributing.

"Are you okay?"

For some reason, that pissed her off. Of course she wasn't okay. But she was here and that might not count very high in his book, but it did in hers. She could have bolted. Was still considering it, but as long as she remained, she'd count this as a good day. She just had to get through this.

"I'm fine," she said brusquely, against her best efforts to sound normal.

His eyebrow lifted and his lips twitched. "Right. I believe that." He dropped his head and lifted his pencil to the paper and drew the first line.

There was no hesitation in his movements. Not where he'd start or what he'd start with. His pencil hit the paper and moved swiftly in sharp strong lines.

She almost hated him for that confidence. That control. He didn't have to feel bad here. She didn't know what Jenna thought this project would do for her or Sean, but she knew Sean wasn't planning on taking it seriously. She wished she felt the same way. She could use a bit of attitude in her life.

She also could use a bit of healing. No, there was no point in fooling herself. She needed a lot more than a little. Realizing this was where she was going to be for the next hour, she closed her eyes and tried to disappear. Until a child's voice interrupted her.

"Hi."

"Hi," Sean said. "What's your name?"

"Jonathon, but you can call me Jon." The bright tone didn't hide the wobbly frailness of the boy's voice.

Robin froze, her heart hiccupping at the boy's name. She didn't want to open her eyes and look, but she couldn't help herself. Her brother's name had been Jonathon.

Peeking through her lashes, she studied Jon. The little boy appeared to be about eight years old, tight black curls covering his head. His face showed some damage, the reconstruction already in progress. He didn't look anything like her brother – thank heavens. That made it easier to gaze upon him. He stood beside Sean, his attention completely absorbed in Sean's movements. At least he'd ignored her. And maybe if she kept her eyes closed, he'd continue to do so.

"Hey, cool," the boy said in awe.

Sean laughed. "What's cool?"

Robin had to open her eyes to see. The little boy was pointing at Sean's picture. From her angle, she couldn't see what he was drawing, it all looked like random black lines. Not to the little boy apparently.

"You're an artist."

"Nah, it's just a hobby."

Robin heard something in his voice that made her look over to study his face. He was resistant to the idea of being an artist for some reason. She'd never seen anything he'd created, but she had to admit that the more he resisted, the more curious she got.

"Are you going to draw us?" He pointed to the nurse. "Andy said you were."

Sean nodded. "Along with Robin here."

Jon looked back at Robin, who dropped her lashes, then over to Sean then back again. "Are we going to see her face?"

Sean looked over at him. "You can't see it?"

"Sure. But I meant the part that she keeps hidden."

"Ask her."

"Nah." He leaned closer and dropped his voice, adding, "She doesn't look friendly." He backed away, shot one final look at Robin, and dashed back to the others.

Robin's gaze followed the child. The room appeared to be males only. Jon grabbed a small plastic car and vroomed it across the floor, completely at ease.

Boys. Thinking of that, she turned to check out what Sean was doing. And found his hand moving like wildfire across a large sketchbook. And she meant like wildfire. She wouldn't be surprised if smoke rose up from the paper. The look of concentration on his face was fascinating.

He was competent, focused…passionate.

She wished she knew what she was supposed to be doing for this project. Sean was supposed to sketching pictures of her *with* the kids. That meant she was supposed to be *with* the kids. Not sitting like a statue at his side. She got that. But how? Better she just stay in the shadows and let him do his thing.

Lord knew that's what she wanted to do – but it hardly seemed fair.

Not that fairness was high on her list of concerns at the

moment.

SEAN WATCHED HIS hand shift across the paper. As if controlled by another's hand. He couldn't be doing this. Or rather, he'd not sketched in this manner before. Then he really hadn't done much sketching, period. He'd joked to himself about giving Jenna stick figures. He'd done some nice stuff before, but not much of it, and he didn't have the time now to do a good job on all of them either. Not in a week. He had no idea how long it would take to complete this report because he didn't have a good grasp of just what he was supposed to be doing. It had been a long time since he'd actually completed any artwork. He was rusty.

He flexed his fingers, seeing the oversized knuckles, the slightly uneven shape. His knuckles were stiff, the fingers aching. He'd never thought to hold a pencil like this again. His father hated to see him with a sketchbook and pencil. The punishments had been severe. Memories flooded his psyche. His father, going into rage, grabbing his hands followed by that horrible crisp snapping sound... Broken pencils...broken fingers...broken dreams.

Easing his gaze from the image in front of him, he looked up and glanced down the room, catching Jon's sharp features, his quirky grin, his guileless eyes. His hand never hesitated.

If he was superstitious, he'd have tossed the paper away or better yet, burned it. But he'd started the picture consciously. He remembered making that decision to start on the right-hand side of the page center but slightly lower. He just didn't remember much else. That was because he'd been busy watching Robin.

Emotions swamped him, and his hand slowed. He shaded the shadow side of Jon's face, added a rough patch to his elbow. Thickened a wrinkle on his shirt.

His mind turned over what he'd seen. What he'd felt. What he'd witnessed. And they'd only been here for an hour...

CHAPTER 8

ROBIN TRIED TO stay in the same place and watch the children. Tried but failed. Inside it was as if a scab she'd placed over her painful memories had been ripped off before the wound had a chance to heal. Memories of families. Memories of her brother. Of laughter. Of pain. Of being normal. Of never going to be normal again.

If she let it, the pain would cripple her. Send her back to a dangerous time if she wasn't careful. She'd had no family to hold her to reassure her that all would be well. No familiar face smiling lovingly at her. No loving voices telling her she'd be okay. She had always woken up alone, reliving the loss of her family each and every time.

She rubbed her eyes at the reality of her situation. She was alone. Right now, surrounded by children as she was, she'd never felt more lonely.

"It doesn't make any sense," she whispered.

There was a sudden stillness beside her. She glanced over at Sean, realizing he'd heard her. And his hand had stopped.

Hence the odd silence. The odd scratching sound had been going on in the background. A low level grating noise she'd barely noticed…until it stopped.

She wanted to look at his pictures, but for the same reason she didn't want to see any of it. She was scared he was sketching something she wasn't. But she was more scared that he'd see more than she wanted him to see and sketch exactly what she was.

A coward.

"Can we leave yet," she said in a harsh whisper.

Sean looked at her then cast a quick glance around the room before dropping his gaze to the page. "I'm almost finished."

She nodded but kept her eyes averted. How long had they been here? How long were they supposed to stay? She had no idea what arrangements Jenna had made.

"Okay. We're good." Sean stood up. The sound of his chair being pushed back pulled her out of her reverie. She stood up quickly, almost knocking her chair over. She hated her awkwardness. Hated the return of that instinct to run. That need to get the hell away.

Then as if a herd of elephants were rushing toward her, she realized several kids had raced toward them.

A fine tremor rippled through her. A faint film rose on her skin. And her breath caught in the back of her throat. She needed to get out of here.

Now.

SEAN WATCHED ROBIN escape from the room ahead of the kids. Again. It seemed like her normal defense when a situation became untenable. And apparently a group of kids was untenable. He packed up his pencils and tossed the bag over his shoulder as he was suddenly surrounded by the group of boys. "Goodbye guys."

"Bye," came a chorus from around him.

"Can we see the picture?"

He laughed. "I'll show you on our next visit."

"K."

"Are you coming back tomorrow?"

"Yes." That last question came from Jon. Sean grinned and waved at him. "See you tomorrow."

And he walked out. He had no idea where Robin had gone, but there were few places she could go. As it was, he found her waiting by the elevators, leaning against the wall with her eyes closed.

"Ready?"

She nodded but didn't look at him.

Silently, they moved downstairs and out to the parking lot. She got in with no trouble, almost uncaring, as if she was bothered by something much bigger.

He had no idea what. Or why. And was running short on empathy at this point. They'd both faced a few demons today. He couldn't believe the drawings he'd been working on. He was on a high. She was on a low.

Somewhere there had to be a meeting ground. Surely.

Instinctively, he stared down at his fingers and flexed them. Maybe the long break from sketching had actually helped his skill level improve.

He started the engine and drove back to the hotel. He checked the time. It was after 4pm already. They'd ended up being at the hospital for three hours. It had seemed to be half that time. A quick glance at Robin's clenched fists and he realized that for her, it had likely seemed twice as long as it had been.

Just minutes from the vibrant core of Vancouver city and only a few blocks from the hotel, he said, "Feel better?"

She never answered. He looked over to see her staring straight ahead, her face blank.

"Robin?"

No answer.

He really didn't know how if he should push or not. He was working on it but hated to get involved. Given a chance, he avoided people. Avoided attachments. He was a loner by choice.

So what the hell had happened to him that he was even caring enough to ask?

He pulled into the parking lot and turned off the engine. He turned to Robin, who still sat motionless. "Look, today must have been tough on you. I don't know what happened to scare you back inside yourself, but obviously something did. If you don't want to talk to me – fine. Then talk to Jenna at least. Talk to someone."

Slowly, she turned her head and stared at him. He winced at the bruised look on her face, the moisture glisten-ing in the corner of her eye, and had a powerful want to know what had caused it.

And she had a powerful need to say it. To give voice to that agony inside, to admit it existed. To give it life that she couldn't.

His gut twisted. But not for him.

He'd been there before. Figured to never return but watching her…God, it brought up all of his own shit. Ha. Determinedly, he squashed that back down deep into his psyche.

So many people gave into their fear. And when fear took over, they lost the ability to fight. Then it was over before it started.

Something Robin appeared to have done.

He'd used anger to solve his problems. Not any better than Robin's method, but preferable as it empowered him. It was, however, difficult to control. Giving into the anger blinded him. And if he got in too deep, the rage made him incapable of rational reason – something he had to be mindful of. Still, anger had gotten him through the worst times of his life.

That it was just a front for the real problems didn't matter. This system worked for him.

Robin didn't appear to have an angry bone in her.

Forgiveness was the only way forward for both of them.

Robin might manage it in her lifetime.

In his…fuck that.

"Let's get you inside. Maybe a hot shower before dinner will help."

He hopped out and walked around the truck. He opened her door and nudged her forward. Silently, they moved through the hotel until Robin stepped into her room and locked the door. Standing outside, Sean heard the snick of the lock. Good. He walked toward his room, his cell phone already in his hand. Once inside, he called Jenna.

CHAPTER 9

ROBIN WAITED UNTIL she heard Sean's footsteps head back down the hallway. She collapsed backwards on her bed.

"Damn it."

She wanted to quit. Just walk away and count this as a bad deal. One she couldn't deal with. She'd tried and it didn't work. So she'd walk away. Try again another day. Another year maybe. Because that's how long it would be before she tried something like this again.

There was a knock on the door.

She ignored it.

The knock came again. "Robin? It's Jenna."

She groaned. She didn't need this. She wasn't ready. Everything was too raw. Too vulnerable.

"Robin, I'm not going to go away."

"Damn it."

She got up off the bed and walked to the door. She unlocked it and opened it to face her. "I'm tired."

"And stressed, and you've had a shock."

Jenna's voice was gentle. Caring.

Tears filled her eyes. She shook her head and backed into her room. Jenna followed. Robin sat down on the edge of her bed. She brushed away the tears. Jenna sat down beside her. Close but not touching. Robin desperately wanted a hug but knew it would be her undoing. "Tell me what happened."

"Nothing happened," she cried. "I sat there for hours in complete silence locked away in fear." She threw up her hands in defeat.

"Of the children?"

"I don't know. First the truck ride…maybe that started it." She tried to sort it out in her head, but it was still so dead inside. Unclear. Like walking through a fog. Or a land mine. She could never quite forget that Jenna would be analyzing everything she said. She gave a broken laugh. Then again, that's what she'd come here for.

"The hospital was the next button. The smell…it got to me immediately and after that, it got worse. I felt as if I walked through quicksand, going deeper and deeper with every step." She closed her eyes, hating the trip back through her miserable day. "I shut down before I got into the ward."

"So you went in afraid and expecting the worst."

Robin lifted her head to gaze at Jenna. "How could I not? You know the last time kids saw my face, they ran screaming from me."

Jenna smiled gently. "And did it happen today?"

A broken laugh escaped. "I didn't let it. I never let anyone see me." She shook her head in an exaggerated movement, highlighting the hairstyle across her face. "I kept my back to everyone, said nothing, and was the basic living statue you'd see on any street corner." She frowned at Jenna, finally understanding. "So no, it didn't."

"So then it was different than last time."

"Not really," Robin defended herself. "It was just as bad."

"Was it though?" Jenna was gently persistent. "Not really. You weren't laughed at. The children didn't mock you. They didn't run from you in terror."

"But I still hated it," Robin cried. "And it could have happened."

"Sure, but you hated it *because* you were expecting a disaster. Waiting for it to happen."

Robin swallowed and tried to stare back defiantly and couldn't quite make it. It took several tries then finally she managed to clear her dry throat. "You don't know what it was like…the fear choking me to the point where I can't see or hear or feel anything."

"I do understand." Jenna reached out a hand and gently rubbed her shoulder. "The thing is, you went there. On your own."

"And failed," she said bitterly. "Miserably."

"Oh no! Not at all," Jenna exclaimed. "Don't ever think that."

Robin threw herself backwards on the bed. "Are you kidding? That's the only thing you could call this. It was terrible. Publicly visible in body, but definitely concealing my face and hiding out, completely terrorized, inside."

"What did the kids do?"

"Nothing," she cried. "They did nothing."

"Nothing? As in they didn't speak to you? They crowded about Sean or they took off and did their own thing?"

Robin closed her eyes and tried to remember exactly what had happened. "They stayed down at their end, then I turned my back on them and didn't see anything else. After a while, a little boy walked over to see what Sean was doing. He was a big enough shock. I couldn't look at the others after him, so I have no idea if they were looking at me." She shrugged. "But everyone does."

"And if everyone does, why wear your hair like that? Why not pull it back so they can see? Then they will see and finally stop trying to look."

"Not likely." Robin ran her hands over her face. "That's not the way it works. They look but because they can't get close enough to really see enough, and because it's not polite to stare, they constantly try to get a clearer look. It's like always being under watchful eyes. As if they're waiting for me to give them all a chance to see just how bad the damage is."

"If it's just children, then let them. They will be honest. They will exclaim and ooh and aah, maybe cry out a little, and they will get over it."

"I'm sure they will – eventually. But in the meantime, they will scream and have night terrors. I can't be responsible for that!" She shuddered and swiped at the tears dripping down her cheeks. "I couldn't sleep for months after those kids ran screaming from me."

"But that was then. This is now," Jenna said firmly. "Your face has progressed from that time, and you're a different person."

"No," Robin replied. "I'm not. I'm still a monster."

SEAN SAT IN the dining room and brooded. No one came close. Good thing. He had no idea what he was supposed to do about Robin. He hoped he'd done the right thing by calling Jenna. That's what she was here for. That's what they were all here for. By rights he should be rejoicing that Robin had a breakthrough…or something. He just hoped it didn't break Robin.

In a black mood, he ordered a beer and sat quietly in the

corner and drank. He should have food, but he wasn't hungry. He felt like he should have done more. But she wouldn't talk to him, so what more could he do? That's why he didn't like people clogging up his life. They were complications he didn't want.

And he wouldn't have let Robin get under his skin if it wasn't for the constant reminders about Paris. He'd have known how to help his sister. Robin was a stranger. Less of one now than she had been earlier, but still a stranger in many ways. Or rather, he felt he understood her more because of Paris, but she'd consider *him* a stranger. And that was a different story.

A plate of roast beef and veggies arrived in front of him. He looked up at the waitress in surprise. "I didn't order this."

"Jenna ordered it for you," she said with a smile. "I'll bring your salad in a moment."

Surprised, he watched her stop by another table and take their order. The smells wafting up from his plate smelled great. He was hungry. The food would go a long ways to help fill him up. The emotional pit wouldn't be so easy to fill, but at least he finally admitted that maybe the pit needed filling.

He took his first bite and smiled as Jenna sat down at the seat opposite him. "Thanks for dinner."

"Thanks for the heads up on Robin."

That took some of his appetite away. He stared down at his meal and asked in a low voice, "How is she?"

"Better now. Recuperating."

"She should eat," he said, forking up a bite. "It's been a long day."

"True. She might come down."

He studied the prof's beautiful face then shook his head. "You don't believe that."

"Well, I hope she does, but if she doesn't feel like being around other people, she can always order room service."

"True." He pondered that. "It would be better if she came down."

Jenna's head tilted in acknowledgement. "That doesn't mean she can do more today." With a gentle smile, Jenna stood up and left.

He watched her slim figure sway between the other tables on her way out. He'd love to know her story. She was one attractive woman. And very empathetic. He didn't think that came easily. In fact, he highly suspected she'd gone through her own hell and had somehow come out the other side clean and intact, ready to help others.

Speaking of others…he pulled out his phone to text his sister when it buzzed in his hand. Paris. Of course, being twins, things like that happened all the time.

How is it?

He raised his eyebrows at that simplified phrase. Of course she meant the workshop. But what could he tell her? He texted back. *Fine.*

Such a simple answer, but what else was he supposed to say? That someone around him had a major breakdown and the process so painful and disturbing he wished he hadn't seen it? At the same time, he knew things were changing. Inside. Outside. He couldn't explain it, but the solid center he'd been standing on was…gone.

That it might be a good thing didn't change the discomfort of it.

The next text from his sister said, *Are you learning anything? How do you think the workshop would be for me?*

And that made him wince.

She'd likely do very well here. He didn't know why Jenna had suggested another session down the road would be more helpful, but he had to admit he didn't know how Paris would handle stressors like Robin had today.

Paris usually went all out or all in. There were no half measures for her. And although strong and caring, she was so very afraid inside.

He was hesitant as to what to tell her. How did he explain that for some, it was painful to be here? For others, like him, it was painful to watch others go through their stuff. And have his own issues flare. It was easy to stomp those issues back down deep inside for the moment, but it could get harder to keep a lid on them if the chain reaction of events speeds up.

He ordered another beer and stared out of the window, only just now realizing he'd picked the same corner of the dining room that Robin had earlier. He sat in the far corner, his back to the wall where he could watch the world go by. Like Robin had watched the world go by.

What was he going to do about her? A connection had formed between them, whether she was aware of it or not. Should he go and see her tonight or did he leave her alone and see how she was in the morning? He had no idea if the project was off...and a part of him would be relieved, yet another part would feel disappointed. He'd caught a glimpse of something he wanted for himself.

To free his inner artist.

He'd sketched like a demon today. He hadn't expected that. He had seen something in those kids' faces that had tore at his heart yet he'd managed to capture much of their uniqueness on paper – at least of Jon. He didn't need someone else to tell him the images were good, he knew they were. He could see it. He'd been waiting to see Robin's reaction to his drawings, but as she'd locked herself up inside, he doubted she'd even seen them.

He put down his beer bottle and went to stand up when he saw her.

Robin. Dressed in black, her skin whiter than usual, with shadows under her eyes and her shoulders straight. She was facing the world. She'd taken a hit, ran away, and was now back again. Interested, he sat down and waited to see what she'd do. This had been her pattern all day. He'd wondered where she'd learned to take the hit and still get back up – or was that a natural characteristic? It was something Paris had never learned. She'd taken the hit and stayed down out of striking distance.

Whereas for him, he'd taken the hit, but it had been a matter of pride to not go down. And if his legs were knocked out from under him, he'd jumped back up.

Robin strode into the room with a casual controlled air. But the furtive glances at the other occupants said much to her state of mind. The controlled mantle was in place, but it was thin. Too thin. He waited for her to see him. She was heading straight for him. Or for her spot.

She looked up, saw him, and her steps faltered.

He smiled at her. "Glad to see you're feeling better."

She made a small motion with her hand. "A nap helped."

No doubt it would, but he highly doubted that she'd had one.

"Do you want this spot?" He stood up and motioned to his seat.

Her lips quirked. "Thanks, but I'll be fine on this side." And she slid into the seat across from him.

CHAPTER 10

ROBIN STUDIED SEAN'S face, noting the relief in his eyes. Had he been worried about her? To that extent? Surely not. He didn't know her. Then again, he'd been with her at the hospital. Seen her reaction.

She turned her gaze to look out the window. It was overcast and growing darker by the minute. Vancouver was known for its wet gray skies. Still, the summer had been good to them and the plants did need a regular amount of rain, so it was hard to complain. Besides, it suited her mood perfectly.

So why that compulsion to come down to the restaurant? She could have stayed safely hidden away in her room.

Lost as she was, she barely registered the voices beside her. She pulled herself back to hear Sean asking for a menu for her. She shook her head. "I'm not hungry."

He overruled her. "Bring her a bowl of soup and a salad please."

She stared at him in bemusement. Normally she'd have been pissed. Today, that required too much energy. "That's going to get you into trouble, you know."

He raised his beer bottle and took a healthy swig, but he kept his eyes on her.

"What is?" he asked when he could.

"Being a protector."

His eyebrows shot up. She wondered if he had any idea how often he reacted like that. Or if it was only with her.

"I'm hardly a protector."

"Except that's exactly what you are. You kept everyone away at the hospital," she gave him a crooked smile. "Brought me home even though I was barely functioning, and then when I was safely in my room, you contacted Jenna to let her know I was in trouble."

He put the bottle on the table a little harder than necessary. "I only did what anyone would do."

"Really?"

The waitress returned just then to set a full bowl of some kind of cream soup in front of her and salad to the side.

Robin nodded toward the light meal in front of her. "Most people would not order me a meal."

"Well, someone did the same for me tonight, so I'm just passing it on."

But those eyes of his were watchful. Assessing.

"I'm fine you know." At least she was better than she had been. "It was a tough day, but I'm feeling more in control."

His gaze narrowed slightly but didn't ease back. It was as if he was probing to the very depths of her. She couldn't tear her gaze away. Somehow the tenor of the glance shifted from probing and distant to heating up, a shortening of that gaze so they were almost connected. It was…intimate.

She tried to pull her gaze away and couldn't. He held her completely in his power.

And yet instead of being nervous or uncertain, she felt…comforted and so very aware of him.

"Definitely a protector," she whispered, her insides tightening with a slow heat. Did he feel it? She searched his eyes, looking for an answering awareness in his gaze.

Instead, he lowered his gaze, effectively breaking the contact.

And left her feeling bereft. Shuddering from the shock to her system, she picked up her spoon and tasted her soup. Clam chowder. Delighted, she ate until there wasn't a drop left. Feeling replete and still with a salad to round out the edges, she sat back with a happy smile.

"Thank you," she said sincerely. "That was delicious."

"Apparently." He motioned to the well-cleaned out dish. "You look like you could eat a second one."

"No," she laughed, "I'll be lucky if I can eat the salad."

"Well, go for it." He slumped back with a half smile on his face. She eyed him carefully then shrugged and lifted the first forkful of the greens. She barely held back a moan. "Even this tastes wonderful. I don't know what happened but my taste buds seem amplified."

"Maybe it's all that emotional stuff."

"Stuff?" She grinned as she popped another bite in, then mumbled, "Maybe."

It took only a few minutes to polish the salad off as well. When it was done, she stared down at her empty plate almost in dismay. "Regardless of the reason, I'm grateful. I haven't enjoyed a meal so much in a long time."

"Good. Now a good night's sleep and you'll be ready to face tomorrow."

She wrinkled her face at him. "You just had to remind me, didn't you?"

His lips twitched. "As we have a long week ahead, it helps to keep everything clear."

She nodded. "Probably. That doesn't make it easier to deal with." Neither did it help her stomach digest a wonderful meal that was starting to lose its astonishing taste. Her stomach started to sour. But the truth was the truth. "And considering that, I think I'll head to my room and try and get some rest before I have to face that mess all over again."

She stood up. He stood up with her. "I'll walk you back up. I'm going to my room also."

"It's early. There's probably some evening session happening here with Jenna." Not that she planned on going. She'd had as much shake up as she could handle for one day. She caught the shift in his features. She stopped to study him. "You have no intention of going, do you?"

At the slight shake of his head, she had to ask, "Why are you even here? It's not to learn – that's obvious."

He nudged her gently out of the way as several people tried to walk past. Then he led her toward the bank of elevators. The same group from the restaurant was also getting on, so there was neither room to maneuver nor any privacy to speak. At the fourth floor, they got out and he walked her down to her door. There he stopped, took the card from her hand, and unlocked it. He pushed it open and motioned for her to enter.

"How did you know my room number? Earlier I mean, when you brought me back here from the hospital." It just hit her. She hadn't told him. So how had he known?

"My room is next door."

HE WATCHED CONFUSED interest whisper across her face. She stepped back to glance down the hallway as if looking for his room. He pointed to the door slightly down from hers.

She nodded, gave him a quick smile, and closed the door

in his face. He heard the snick of the lock.

As a message, it was pretty clear. He walked to his room and entered. Tossing his key on the dresser, he pulled out his cell phone and called his sister.

"Hey, I'm so happy to hear from you," Paris said. "Now spill. How's it going?"

He brought her up to date, minimizing Robin's afternoon.

"She'll feel better tomorrow," she said. "It's hard at the time but afterwards it's such a better place to be in."

"As long as she can do this day after day. We have to go several more times."

"Well, I hope she can for your sake. You need to work on your own issues."

"What issues?" he scoffed. "I don't have any." At least none he planned to work on here.

"How about your inability to let anyone close?"

"What inability?" He frowned. "I don't know what you're talking about."

"Yes, you do," she said sadly. "You don't trust anyone. You *won't* trust anyone."

He pulled his shirt off and tossed it over the chair. His shoulder ached from clutching the pencil today. Not that his shoulder needed a reason to scream. That was the weakest part of his body. Once an abuser knew your weakness, he had control over you. He looked at the mass of scar tissue that completely deformed the joint. And saw his father's bloodshot eyes, that grotesque look of hatred in his eyes, and that unholy light of joy as he dug his thumbs hard into the damaged joint...and jerked the ball free...again...

"Sean, you there?"

Shaking as the memories sent a shard of pain down his

shoulder and chest, sweat breaking out across his forehead, Sean cleared his throat and said, "Yeah, well. Maybe I'm just always meant to be alone."

"No," his sister cried. "You aren't. None of us are meant to journey this way."

"How do you know?" he asked in a serious tone. Holding the phone tucked between his neck and shoulder, he closed his eyes, the painful memories receding, and let his fingers massage deep into the knots, loosening the tightness of his injured joint.

While the pain eased, he considered the work he'd done today. The sketching had been intense. More than he'd thought. He'd never felt so gripped in the middle of drawing like that before.

Had never thought to experience such passion for his art.

He finished his call to Paris and hung up the phone. There was a pool in the hotel. He should go and do a few laps then sink into the hot tub. The heat would do wonders for his sore muscles. That and a good night's sleep and his arm would be as good as new for tomorrow.

He checked the time. It was after 8pm. Would the pool be still open? He needed to find out. His physical health was one thing he couldn't afford to let go. It only took a couple of minutes to change. He grabbed the spare towel in the bathroom, his key card, and walked out.

There were a couple of people doing laps in the pool and several more in the hot tub. Well, maybe the hot tub would be cleared by the time he finished his laps. He dropped his towel and dove into an empty lane. Doing the front crawl, he could feel his shoulder pull and pinch with every lift. He knew this routine and settled in for a long swim. He lost track of his laps, instead going by the fatigue level in his body.

When he figured he'd done enough, he pulled himself out of the water and sat at the edge for a long moment, giving his trembling muscles a moment to calm down. He took a deep breath and stood up, realizing just how tired he was. He'd overdone the swimming tonight. Instead of being strong and refreshed by morning, he was likely to be tired and sore. Not smart.

The pool had emptied and even the hot tub was down to just one person.

He slowly walked over. He was tired now, his arm sore and throbbing. At the hot tub, he dropped into the water and sank until only his head was above. And let the heat work its magic. He closed his eyes and rested.

Afterwards, he'd blame his fatigue for not noticing the odd silence. When he did finally realize the atmosphere around him was pregnant with something unusual, he sat up on the bench under the water to look around.

The shocked gasp had him turning his head. And he gazed directly into Robin's horrified face.

While she stared at his damaged shoulder, he couldn't help but stare at her damaged face.

CHAPTER 11

ROBIN HAD SEEN one person swimming when she'd entered the pool area. But after realizing that the hot tub was empty, she'd made the decision to stay. She really wanted to soak. Her insides felt wrung out. Her muscles were achy, and the injured side of her face throbbed from clenching her jaw. The stress was killing her, even now that it had slid down to manageable levels. She could have tried to go to sleep, but just the thought had sent her nerves tightening. She was afraid the nightmares would return.

After lowering herself into the warm water and feeling her muscles soften and relax, she knew she'd done the right thing. She sank completely under the water, letting the heat soak into the muscles and skin of her face and head. Alone, she could relax and not worry about prying eyes.

Until Sean had arrived.

Why him?

Why now?

But as always, there was no answer. She could only stare at him in shock. Dear God. She'd seen the small scars on his hand, his fingers, his neck. The tiny portion that showed under his shirt.

There was no way she could have guessed at the rest.

No one could have.

His right shoulder was shiny and rippled with the mixed

of damaged and healed tissue trying to live peacefully together. There had to be some injury to the actual joint from the grotesque look of the pitted muscles. Her heart softened, ached. Damn. What he must have gone through…

Her gaze wandered his wide chest, seeing the small burn-like scars, cuts that had been too big or too deep to heal without proper care. So many of them. She knew his back was likely worse.

"I'm so sorry," she whispered.

He jerked slightly, then sat up and glared at her, giving her a clearer view of his chest.

And she knew.

"You said you were abused as a child." She shook her head. "That's a lie." There was no other way to say it. But she tried. In fact, the words spurted out on their volition. "You look like you were tortured on a daily basis for years."

"Apparently," he said carelessly, the tone of his voice mocking. Distant. And she understood.

She couldn't help it – tears burned the back of her eyes. She blinked them back furiously, then realizing that wasn't going to be enough, she dipped her hands in the water and gently bathed her face, trying to hold her emotions back. It was the last thing he'd want. *That* she understood. Sympathy was one thing. Pity – quite another.

When she could, she straightened and looked over at him again. He'd leaned his head back and closed his eyes, letting the bubbles come up to cover the rest of him. It didn't matter. She'd seen enough of his body to know he must have had a horrible childhood. And he'd survived. Thrived even. But now she understood the mocking cynical edge to his voice, that glare in his eyes, that hidden sense of having seen the worst people could offer. That power of no longer giving a damn.

Feeling the pain welling up again, she sank below the water, reveling as the warmth closed over her face. Soothing her stinging eyes.

When she surfaced again, she settled back down against the back of the hot tub and wondered at him being able to go to the children's hospital so easily. She snuck another glance over at him. Lord, she ached as she looked at him. And she thought she had it bad.

Talk about a reality check.

HE HATED THE shocked look on her face. He thought he was immune to seeing that. Especially on a woman. Hence keeping relationships at a distance. He'd had enough one-night stands to know he needed to cover up in the morning before the women saw the details in daylight. Most weren't likely to care as it was always dark and they'd been there for their own needs. There'd been no emotion involved. But he'd seen enough revulsion on some faces to keep that sense of distance.

Screw them all.

As he lay there relaxed, letting his body soak up the warmth, he let his mind dwell on what he'd seen of her face. Compared to his shoulder, he didn't think it was bad. Still, for a woman, it was a part of her body that was so very visible. The scars, the twist to the corner of her eye, the sunken cheek where the muscle underneath had been damaged would be hard to hide.

He could see work had been done. And more was needed. He didn't know if she was in between surgeries or they'd done what they could. At least for now. She hadn't clarified that point.

The look of his shoulder was nothing. It was functional and that's what mattered. He no longer cared what anyone thought. At least he tried not to. In the summer, at the beach, he covered up for other people's sake. To avoid making them uncomfortable. To avoid the inevitable questions.

Especially for Paris. The sight of his back, his body, never failed to bring tears to her eyes.

He'd do anything to avoid hurting her.

He opened his eyes to study Robin, watching as her face broke through the water, her hair streaming behind her. From his position, he could see the hairline behind her cheek was further back, her ear disfigured, and the cheekbone covered with bright shiny skin. She was still healing.

He could only imagine the trauma Robin had already gone through.

His gaze wandered downward to the pink angry streak down her neck and realized as he studied her shoulders – she was likely as badly scarred as he was. She wore a modest one-piece bathing suit. It couldn't begin to cover her injuries. He doubted she went swimming in public. It said much about her day that she was here at all.

He didn't give a damn about his scars.

And she likely cared too much.

He'd been like this since forever. And knew that it was the price of survival. Besides, what was the alternative? He suspected from the look of the scar tissue on her face that this was a fairly recent development in her life. "Have you ever been married? Engaged?"

Oh shit. Where the hell had that had come from? He sank a little lower in the water. Not that he could go much deeper and still breathe. "You don't have to answer that. It just popped out."

"No," she said, "I've never been married or engaged. Came close a time or two, but it didn't work out."

"Ah," he muttered. Christ, he sounded like a dolt. He should just shut the hell up. He didn't do small talk. Or relationships.

"Not an issue," she murmured quietly. "I haven't had time for relationships since the accident."

Ah, this was the first time she'd mentioned that. Dare he ask? But curiosity got the better of him. "How long ago was the accident?"

"Almost six years now," she said absentmindedly.

At least her voice said it wasn't an issue any longer. Likely she'd had a normal childhood, happy and stable, before her world blew apart. Yeah, life was like that. "That must have been tough."

"Yep. But not as bad as a lifetime of abuse. I was happy and settled and thought I was heading forward in life. Had a long term relationship with dreams of that whole house, white picket fence and the perfect two kids."

"And what happened?"

There was silence, then she sighed heavily. "I found out that the perfect dream requires two perfect people, not one that is badly damaged."

The sadness in her voice got to him. There were layers of emotion in her tone. Old and new. He could understand that the dream might need to be changed. But it didn't have to be discarded completely.

CHAPTER 12

ROBIN SETTLED BACK into the water. Waves of depression washed through her.

Just the reminder of all those long evenings talking and planning out her future – her imaginary future with boyfriends and girlfriends over the years. How sad. She missed those hopes and dreams the most. It didn't need to be as bad as it felt to her – she knew that.

At least, she'd been told that many times. However, to know she was supposed to feel something other than what she did made her feel worse. Like how wrong was that? Just because people said something was right didn't make it true. Only she wanted them to be right. She wanted to be able to look forward and see sunshine and roses. A life full of laughter and love. Where children didn't run from her and men didn't cringe when they saw her.

But dreaming a dream didn't make it a reality.

"Thoughts?"

She gave a broken laugh. "Not worth repeating."

"Ah. Stuck in that self-pity mode, huh?"

She froze. How dare he? She opened her eyes and glared at him. "What do you know?" she said bitterly. The words were flying out before she had a chance to hold them back. Damn. Because he of course did know. Just in a different way. Groaning, she closed her eyes and sank back, muttering,

"Sorry."

"Why? Because you think it's not fair to lash out when you're hurting? It's not, but haven't you heard that life isn't fair?"

Damn him for being so reasonable. She wanted to *really* lash out. She wanted to hit him – have him be a target that she could pour her anger and frustration out on. But what good would it do other than be a temporary release of the emotional stress building inside? Besides, he'd already learned life wasn't fair. She had no business feeling sorry for her lot in life when his had been so much worse. She'd been loved while young, had grown up in a nurturing environment, her every need cared for.

And him…she wondered if he had any good memories or if it was all one black pit of pain and despair. His situation made her angry on so many levels. That it stopped her from feeling justified in her own anger and pain was just one of the less nice ones. She hated being petty and selfish. Sure, she had it rough, but as she'd seen today, some of those kids at the hospital had it rough, too. Some people never survived the horrors of their lives. Then there were people like Sean who'd survived – but at what cost?

"There's nothing I can say…" Sean said. "That someone else hasn't already said,"

She opened her eyes and stared. "You are right there."

"So I won't. It's normal to feel angry, depressed even, but from what I have seen of you – you are anything but normal."

That she hadn't expected. Nor did it please her to hear it. After all like he'd said – the little bit of her that he'd seen…wasn't much. And not enough to judge her. Good or bad. "You know nothing."

"And you're going to make sure that I don't know any more, right? Use anger to keep others away. Keep your pride intact, thinking what the hell, it's all you have left anyways, might as well use it, right?"

She swallowed the hard truths, her mind locking onto his angry comment. Had he done that? Was she doing that? Was pride all she had left? True, pride that kept her head high in situations where she'd rather run away, but it wasn't pride that had kept her hiding away at home, too scared to deal with more of the public than she had to. Where had her pride been then? In hiding with the rest of her.

"Ha," she said defiantly, "You don't know me."

She watched his lip curl, feeling her anger blaze inside. She clenched her fists. As soon as she realized what she'd done, she shoved them under the foaming water, a shudder working its way down her thin frame. She had to regain control. She'd leave, but she didn't know that she had enough spine to walk out of the water. It had been hard enough coming here as it were. She only managed it as she knew the hot tub had been empty.

It had been that philosophy that had gotten her through most public meetings. People were curious, sometimes sympathetic, but they weren't part of her life. She whispered under her breath, "Everyone is just grateful that they don't look like me."

"Isn't that too cynical of an attitude for someone your age?"

She opened her eyes to see Sean staring at her. It wasn't disapproval she was seeing in his eyes, but they were dark with something. And she realized he'd heard her. Heat flushed over her cheeks. "Sorry, I didn't mean to say that."

"You did, you just didn't mean to have me hear your

rambling. Besides, I think you give people too much credit. They aren't thinking about any of that stuff. They just want to do whatever is required for their moral compass to feel comfortable and still be able to get up the next morning and look at themselves in the mirror."

She had to admit, he likely had a better take on humanity than she did. It made her feel oddly more comfortable. As if he really did understand what her life was like.

She wafted her hands around in front of her, her fingers slipping through the foam and bubbles as she contemplated people and humanity.

"How many more surgeries are there to be done?" he asked.

One side of her mouth instinctively twisted downward. "None."

"Meaning there is nothing more the doctors can do for you, or that you won't go for any more surgeries regardless of what the doctors feel they can do?"

The gentle curiosity in his voice threw her off balance. She never had a chance to get to know him because he always showed her a different side of his personality. She knew he didn't like her as a woman – not even a casual one-night stand, but there was something in his demeanor that had been caring. Maybe as one would for a hurt animal. Maybe it was nothing special for her. "I'm done with surgeries."

"Ah." A wealth of understanding laced his voice. She glared at him.

He leaned back and closed his eyes, as if happy to sleep while she was now angry and bitter.

"What? Am I not allowed to say enough?"

"Of course," he said equitably. "After all, why look normal? You can stay angry and bitter this way."

Shocked, she cried out, "That's not fair."

"Life isn't fair, sweetheart, I keep telling you that."

"Then get your own body fixed up. Surely there is something they can do about your shoulder."

"Nope. This is fixed."

She stared at the puckered skin. "It doesn't look it."

"Yeah, but I did the rounds of surgery and this is what I am left with. And you know something – I am okay with that."

She frowned. Surely he couldn't be as blasé about that. Then again, it was his shoulder, and it could be hidden most of the time from prying eyes.

"Doesn't it affect your love life?" She hated the need to know, the curiosity not something she was entirely comfortable with. Had he had the same horrified reaction from women as she'd had from men? That he was comfortable with his body even though he was as disfigured as she was didn't help. In fact, it just added to her off-centeredness.

"Nope. Don't have one to begin with, and if you meant my sex life, then you should have said so, and the answer is still no. The women who I have sex with don't care."

Damn if that didn't leave her stunned, her mind flooding with dozens more questions. He separated love from sex. Whereas she hadn't had sex with anyone she didn't love. Had he loved anyone? Or did he call sex, love? Love was a pathway she didn't expect to go down again. Not after being hurt the last time. She'd carefully wrapped up her bruised heart and packed it away in ice. Like so much of her life.

"What about you? How is the scarring affecting your sex life?"

Really? He'd asked that? Then again, why not? She had.

"My boyfriend and I had been together for two years before my accident. He told me afterwards that there was no way he could have sex with me again. Not even as a mercy fuck."

The crude words left her mouth in a vitriol of pain. She stilled. Oh my God. She hadn't said that, had she? What was it about this man that could set her emotions and her tongue off like that?

She'd never shared Tom's parting words with anyone. Not even to her therapist.

How could she? Tom had been serious. With those few words, he'd broken her heart and driven her self-confidence into a pit deep inside, never to see the light again. After that, she'd iced over her heart to avoid being hurt again.

Until Sean. Why him? Unless it was because he was safe. After this week, she wouldn't have to see him again. Or because he was as broken as she was.

Wincing, she waited for Sean's response, but there was only the effervescence of the water popping gently between them.

"A mercy fuck?' he asked in a delicate voice, humor bouncing from letter to letter.

Closing her eyes, she groaned again, grateful that he couldn't hear her above the bubbles. "That's what he called it."

She stared down at the foam bouncing against her chest, wishing she'd kept her big mouth shut. Then that appeared to be part of this week. Being someone she normally wasn't. Awkward. Scared. Always putting her foot into her mouth and leaving it there. She despaired of the rest of the week given the way it had started. She already wanted to go home. Hide away again. So she wasn't put into these situations. She wanted to go back where she was comfortable. Normal.

Sure, she'd be alone, but that was the reality of her life. This being out in public was like wearing a second skin – one that didn't fit well. She wanted to keep tugging it into place.

And trying to keep her mind focused on the things going on this week wasn't working to avoid the burning sensation on the back of her eyelids. Sean's burning gaze.

After a few moments, the air relaxed slightly and dropped that expectant air. She relaxed back.

"Can't say that I've ever had a mercy fuck."

He said it in such a wondering tone that it caught her funny bone. And against all odds, a surprised giggle escaped. She gasped and opened her eyes to see his big grin.

She couldn't help it. She beamed back and said, "As I turned him down, neither have I."

His belly laugh rolled out free and clean, making her realize that Tom's issues had been just that – his issues. She didn't need to make them hers. And she hadn't realized how his comment had burned. How she'd frozen up on the inside. And how much sharing his comment had freed her.

"Good for you. You are worth so much more than that."

She shook her head and opened her mouth.

"Stop. No more self-degrading comments. You are beautiful. And your beauty is only becoming more obvious as each surgery lets you shine a little brighter."

"And if I chose to not have more surgeries?"

"Then you'll stay just as beautiful as you are now," he said comfortably. He leaned back, dropping his head to the edge of the hot tub. Then added, "You have to go beneath the skin and see the layer underneath."

She pondered that wisdom from another person as scarred as he was. Hard to understand coming from someone with that hard edge he carried around himself like a shield. How could he spout all this stuff and be as messed up as he was?

"If that's true, why are you so touchy about your looks?"

He laughed and barked out, "Because everyone out there is like you – they judge by the covering. I don't want people like that in my life. So I let them see the harder edges so that they won't want anything to do with the inside me."

"Or it's a shield that you use to make sure no one can actually see the real you inside."

"Or that…" he said carelessly. And fell silent.

Somehow she knew that this topic was over. He'd done a lot of work and had made some profound insights. This is who he was.

He was comfortable with himself. As for the rest of the world? He didn't give a damn.

IF THERE WAS ever a guy who deserved punching, Robin's ex was it. A mercy fuck? It boggled the mind and Sean found himself getting pissed all over again. He couldn't help but wonder how much of Robin's issues were caused by his fellow men. Probably too damn many of them.

Then again, all of his had been. His father had been a right bastard. Sean had no memory of the love of his mother, who'd taken off when Paris and he were young, leaving them with their father.

He'd learned. Not fast and not easily. Still, he'd not have survived without his sister. Their bond was strong as they'd been forced to depend on each other for survival.

Something Robin hadn't had. She'd gone from having a loving family who'd always been there for her to being completely alone in an instant. Everything since she'd had to do herself, for herself, by herself.

He couldn't imagine how tough that would have been. How wearying. What happened when she hit a wall and crumpled in defeat? Could she get up and keep going without someone there to help her? Or was that why she struggled for as long as she could then slowly gave up and had gone inside?

Since he'd been an older teen, he'd been fascinated with the psychology of people. Why they did things and what it would take for them to change that behavior. He didn't like many of them, but their behavior fascinated him. He had high hopes for his future once he graduated but had no clue what area he wanted to work in. Maybe profiling. He wouldn't mind helping to put bastards like his father behind bars.

Paris had laughed and said that him taking a psychology course made perfect sense. He was trying to figure out their father.

She was only partly correct. He'd figured out their father. He even understood his mother, she'd been a victim too. But what he was trying to figure out was himself – so he didn't end up like his father.

Deep stuff. He wasn't sure how much progress he'd made. But watching, hearing Robin's struggles made him realize that although the details were different, their journeys were similar.

Not that she'd appreciate hearing that.

Any more than she could handle being told that she was beautiful. She was. In fact, the newly awoken artist in him wanted to grab a pencil right now. It was almost time to go back to their rooms. He had an idea for the report now. He wasn't sure he had the skill to pull it off, but for the first time, he really wanted to try.

His father had tried to separate Sean from his art. He hadn't completely succeeded. But neither had Sean been able to do much since. It had taken Jenna to bring that spark back to life. Who'd have thought?

CHAPTER 13

ROBIN WOKE THE next morning groggy and tired. Talk about a shitty night. When she needed a sound sleep, life had given her a crappy wake up every hour on the hour, only to finally fall into a deeply disturbed sleep at 5am. Like what a joke. She needed her defenses strong today. Of course, this way she'd have little resistance against the world and maybe that would be a good thing – it could shake things up.

Things she wasn't ready to shake up.

She winced. And said out loud, "That's why you're here, idiot." And that couldn't happen while her defenses were strong. This way sometimes, things would slip under her weakened guard and prick her where she needed it most.

A horrible thought. God, she'd be glad when this week was over.

She rubbed her eyes and lay still contemplating the day ahead. She had to go back and see the kids.

It had to get easier. Her chest constricted in dread. They were just kids for Christ's sake. These kids were traumatized enough. And was she supposed to let them see her as she really was and face their horror? Was that the lesson Jenna wanted her to learn? Cause that just sucked big time. She'd already faced that reaction. Look what little good that had done – she'd run away as far as she could to get away. Then had been unable to get out. She was out now. Because of this seminar.

The last thing she wanted was to go back into hiding again.

Yet there was already a thin steel rod of stress running through her. She could feel the slight vibration, that inner shakiness that said her stress levels were rising. She wanted to be able to let the kids see her as she really was, but she couldn't. Not really. And there was no way she'd be able to smile at them as if everything were okay. Nothing was okay. And coming here had just magnified that. Especially after meeting Jon. Just hearing his name hurt.

Jonathon. She missed him so much.

So many buttons pushed already this week, and it was early in the week…

She was going to be a different person by the end of the week. It remained to be seen if that was a good thing or not.

There was a knock on the door. She frowned but threw back her covers, and just dressed in her cami and underwear, she approached the door. "Hello?"

"It's me," Sean said from the other side.

She instinctively opened the door wide enough to peer around the edge. "What's up?"

She studied him, still blinking the sleep out of her eyes. *He* looked great. Like he'd had a dozen hours of sleep. She envied him.

"Breakfast. It's late." He motioned down the hallway. "I wanted to make sure you were up."

"Just." She yawned. "How late is it?"

"Almost 8:45am."

Damn.

"I'll be ready in five." And she slammed the door.

Turning around, she stared bleary-eyed at the room and the tossed up bedding then galvanized into action. She dressed quickly, tossed the bedding back into place with a few quick movements, and rushed out the door. There wasn't even time to eat. And that was also no good. She walked into the seminar late enough that Jenna was already talking to the class. There was only one place left. Beside Sean.

Crap. She slipped into place, hoping to ignore this man who disturbed her too much. He reached over and placed a takeout cup of coffee and a still-warm muffin in front of her.

Oh happy sigh. She might want a break from him, but there was no doubt that a man who would go out of his way to make sure you were awake in time to start the day and then think far enough ahead to make sure you had a hot coffee and a bite to eat was a definite keeper. And the ice around her heart melted a little bit more.

Three hours later, she'd settled into place. Coffee, lectures, a couple of group sessions, and she was feeling more normal. More centered. Nothing had pushed her buttons. It was all good.

She was looking forward to catching up with Tania over lunch. See how her week was going. She'd watched her with the big muscleman Kane a few times and had been worried for her. They'd managed to catch a few private moments to talk so far but that was all. That Tania was still functioning and managing to be relatively calm and normal said a lot about her state of mind. And her progress. Although maybe nothing in her world had blown up – yet.

And just like that, all the thoughts, worries, that sense of increasing dread that she'd worked so hard at keeping under lock and key came flooding back into her mind. She didn't want to go back to the hospital. Didn't want to see those kids. Didn't want to go back out in the world. This hotel was not home, but it was as safe a territory as she could claim here.

In an hour – maybe two – she'd have to leave. And she didn't want to. Didn't dare to. She had no way to know what would happen. But she knew all kinds of horrible things could.

She walked into the dining room when her cell phone went off. She pulled out her phone and stared down at the text message. No, not possible. Everything inside of her revolted.

Sean spoke just then, startling her. "Are you ready? We'll pick up something on the way if you're hungry."

Blindly, she looked around the dining room slowly filling up, her gaze landing on Tania a few tables in front of her. How could she get out of this? Push it back at least another hour. *She wasn't ready*, her mind screamed.

Sean reached out and snagged her arm gently. "Let's go."

And she went.

SEAN HAD READ his text, looked up to locate Robin, and found her frozen in place with her phone in her hand. It was the look of blind panic in her eyes that had gotten to him. She'd been chipper and happy all morning. Too chipper and too happy. He'd watched her interact with the others, getting into the swing of the morning lectures and the smaller group projects. He doubted anyone else had noticed the overloud voice, the over-enthusiastic agreements. The too bright smile. But he had. And he hadn't been able to keep his gaze off of her.

Now she looked to be on the verge of an all-out panic attack. That couldn't happen. He'd never get her to the hospital if she did that.

"What kind of food do you fancy?"

Her voice wooden, she replied, "I couldn't eat a thing."

"I could." His stomach took that opportunity to growl at him. "In fact, I'm going to need to." He kept his hand on her arm and dragged her gently out the front door. As she had her purse with her and as the day was warm, he figured that maybe he could nudge her straight out to his truck. He didn't know what he'd do about food, but it looked like takeout was on the menu. Not that eating and driving was a good idea.

The earlier he got Robin to the hospital, the earlier they could leave. She obviously didn't like this shift in their schedule. He was a roll-with-the punches-kind-of-guy. Paris needed a little more warning.

Like Robin.

He got her outside before she'd realized it. He was glad he'd stashed his art stuff inside the truck already this morning. If he'd had to go and get it now, he'd have a much harder time with her. He also needed food before he started another marathon art session. It was only as he led her to the truck that she baulked. And he remembered how she felt about driving.

Was nothing easy?

"You did fine yesterday. Sure, every time is a new time, but you've got this. In the scale of all the other things you've got to deal with, this one is easy. So let's just do it."

He opened the truck and helped her up onto the seat. He had her buckled in and the door shut before she had a chance to protest. He hopped into the driver's side and made short work of getting the truck out onto the main road.

There was a drive-through sandwich place up ahead. He pulled in and ordered two large subs for the two of them. Realizing it was useless to ask her preferences given her frozen features, he also ordered two bottles of water to go with the meal.

After accepting the food and paying, he did a drive around the block so he could get back onto the road heading in the direction they needed to go.

He checked the dashboard clock. They were going to be a little early. That meant eating in the parking lot.

So be it.

The drive took longer today with the heavy lunch hour traffic. He pulled the truck into the hospital parking lot, found a spot close to where they'd parked yesterday, and shut off the engine. He opened up the bag of food and pulled out a sandwich. He handed it to her. "Eat."

She stared at him and frowned. "I'm not hungry."

"Yes, you are. And your stomach needs this. All that stress and tension is eating away at you from the inside. Give it real food to work on and save the lining of your stomach."

She accepted the sandwich and rested it on her lap. He handed her the bottle of water. Then he pulled out his lunch, opened the wrapping, and took a big bite.

Food. He closed his eyes and let his stomach catch up with the message as he methodically ate his sandwich. He'd missed too many meals in his life to be interested in missing any more.

CHAPTER 14

ROBIN STARED DOWN at the paper-wrapped sandwich then over at Sean. He ate with gusto. Enjoying this moment. This meal. This bite. It didn't take much to realize he was a large appetite kind of guy. He did make the sandwich sound good. She slowly unwrapped hers and peered at the filling. Looked like layers of mixed meat and lots of veggies. Her kind of sandwich. Tempted, she picked it up and took a tentative bite. The aroma of salami and tomato with a hint of mustard caught her nose at the same time as her taste buds sat up and paid attention. It was good. Actually, it was really good.

She didn't realize it but within minutes, she was well into her big sub. She looked sideways and caught Sean staring at her with a big grin on his face. She scowled at him. "What are you looking at?"

"You. Glad to see you're enjoying it."

She glanced down, realized she was almost done, and said, "I am. Thanks."

"No problem." He unscrewed the bottle of water and drained it mostly dry.

She watched one eyebrow rise as he kept pouring down the liquid. She thought she drank a lot of water, but he had her beat in that department.

Afterwards, she finished her sandwich, crumpled up the

wrapper, and popped it back into the bag. She opened her bottle, took a drink, and said, "Okay, let's do this."

She opened her truck door and hopped out while he was still absorbing her words. She didn't wait to see if he followed or not. She heard the truck door open and slam shut followed by long strides hitting the pavement until he was beside her. But he never said a word.

Good. She was taking advantage of a momentary surge of courage to get into the building. With any luck, she'd make it into the damn ward too.

But it wasn't to be. As soon as the elevator doors closed in her face, she could feel her stomach knot up. She swallowed hard. Then again. Under her breath, she repeated, "I can do this. I can do this, I can do this."

"And you can," Sean said quietly at her side. "Easily."

That was when she realized he'd heard her. "I wish I believed you."

He laughed.

She refused to let him get to her. She got that this was easy for him. That he did understand what this trip was doing to her. However, there was nothing funny about it. And *that* was something he should have gotten.

The heavy metal doors slid open. She tensed up inside. Taking a deep breath, she walked forward.

"Have you got some kind of plan of action as to how to handle this today?" Sean asked quietly at her side.

She shot him a sharp look. "Survive."

"How about asking something really small of yourself that would make it an improvement on yesterday?"

She tried to focus on his words. "Like what?"

"Maybe sit facing forward so that the kids can check you out in a different way."

"What good would that do?" She could do it easily enough, but she wasn't sure it would make any difference.

"It's something."

She shrugged. As far as that went, it was a pretty damn small something. Yet her mind caught on the concept. Was there a small step she could take? Regardless of how small, it would be a step in the right direction. Progress was progress…no matter how small.

In the distance, she heard shrieks of laughter covering up the din of quieter screams. The kids.

She stopped in the middle of the hallway. *She couldn't do this.* She went to turn around when she was suddenly jerked off to the one side. She glared at Sean.

"I'm fine."

"Right. That's why you're standing in the way. Come on." He gave her arm a gentle jerk and shifted her in the direction of the kids' ward. "We can get through this."

He walked a half step in front of her, making her feel like she was being dragged. Probably how it looked to everyone else, too. She hated this ball of fear in her stomach that was sinking lower and lower.

Hated that she felt this way. She understood the phrase 'giving away her power' but hadn't really recognized a situation where she'd done just that.

But this was as close as she could imagine it being.

The double doors were in front of them. Sean stopped, gave her a hard look, and said, "Now buck up. We're here. Don't go in there looking like a victim."

Her head snapped back. She glowered at him. "What if that's how I feel?"

"Tough. Deal with it." He surprised her with the harshness of his tone. "I don't care about how you feel right now.

You don't give those kids any more reason to worry than they already have." He reached up and snagged her chin, lifting it to glare into her eyes. "Consider that these visits maybe aren't just about you. Maybe they are for the kids. So give a little – don't just take."

He dropped her chin and strode through the door, his big portfolio banging against the door. She stood in shock and listened to the kids screaming his name. Where had his anger come from? Maybe she had deserved it, but it didn't explain the source.

Then again, she hadn't considered if these visits were causing him stress, too. Jenna had to have a reason for both of them coming here. He was right. She'd been so focused on her problems she hadn't considered the impact of their visits on the kids or the impact on him. Ugh.

Stumbling in the changing landscape of her reality once again, she followed behind him, watching his interaction with the boys. Sure enough when they saw her, they quieted slightly and stepped back a little. Giving her space. And she realized that they weren't so much afraid of her face – they couldn't see it after all – they were more afraid because she was sending out scary vibes.

She was scaring the kids just by her own fear and the walls she'd put up to keep them away.

Talking about seeing a different perspective. She slowly made her way over to the table where Sean was setting up his work. The same little boy, Jon, stood watching at the side of the table. As she approached, he held his ground. Her heart ached. He was so young. And was going through something traumatic from the thin look to him. He was mobile, with crutches, but his hair was too thin and his eyes too big. She'd promised herself she wouldn't focus on any one child –

especially not any one boy – in order to try and keep her sanity. She hadn't expected that one particular boy would focus on her.

Jon's gaze had locked on her face. Watching every move she made. He'd said she was scary yesterday. Maybe she could take one step forward. Not for her sake, for his.

"Hi," she said.

Jon's gaze widened. His gamine grin lit up his face, temporarily pushing the abnormally white skin and heavy black circles under his eyes away. "Hi."

She was disarmed. With a sigh, she sat down on the same chair as she had last time and faced him. Just like Sean had suggested.

SEAN WATCHED ROBIN'S actions from the corner of his eye. He hadn't wanted to be so hard on her, but she'd needed something to snap her out of her mood.

He'd seen some people, namely Paris, frozen by her emotions, but had assumed she was the odd case. Robin was proving that theory to be wrong. He smiled down at the kids who clamored around him, "Give me a moment to unpack, then you can all see the drawing. I did a bit more on it. Maybe if it all goes well today, there will be a couple of other pictures for you to look at soon."

He smiled as several jumped up and raced to the far side of the room as if understanding that he couldn't work if they bugged him.

A couple of the boys stayed behind, quietly watchful as he opened up his portfolio and took out his sketchbook and pencils. He was looking forward to sketching today. The picture had been sitting on the back of his mind, his fingers itching to work on it. In fact, after getting back to his room from the pool, he'd done a bit of work on it. He hadn't planned to, but there'd been something about the little boy that had needed something more. He'd spent only a half hour on it, but the way the boy's eyes look had gone from good to right was perfect. And that was important.

There'd been something in that little boy's gaze. And it hadn't let Sean go until he caught just that look. It bothered him that the space for Robin was blank. He was supposed to be drawing Robin.

Not the boys and Robin, but Robin and the boys. At the moment, he looked to be getting an F on this report.

And he didn't care one bit. He stared around at the kids' faces as he opened the pages to the right place and watched the several heads crowd closer. These kids could use whatever was available to make their day brighter.

He'd been one of them at one time. He understood. More so as these kids likely had family. Friends. Someone who cared for them. He'd watched from the outside. Hurt on the inside. Alone, he'd taken refuge in defiance. Pride. Aggression. It had made it easier to think of the world as one he had to battle. One where he needed to strike out first before he was struck himself.

He sorted through the pencils on the table and turned to a clean page. He started with long lean lightning strokes, trying to capture the sense of the kids staring at them. Their gazes moved with the long strokes of black, as if willing the image to show up clear enough for them to identify what it was. To guess what he was drawing. Then one boy shouted, "Hey, that's Mark."

A little boy leaned forward. "No way, that doesn't look anything like me."

Sean smiled quietly and let his hand add a little shading, thickening the line around the ear, adding a few tufts of hair.

Mark said, "Hey, it is me. That's so cool."

"Do me. Can you draw me too?" asked Jon, his voice weak, his body frail compared to the two robust boys he stood with. Sean glanced up, caught the wistful look in the boy's eyes, and his heart ached a little. No wonder this little guy affected Robin so deeply. "Sure," he said, "I'll give it a try."

He shifted to a different corner of the page and with a softer stroke, he quickly sketched in several curls a small upturned nose, freckles, and the long scrawny neck. It was the look in this boy's eyes Sean wanted to capture. The lost, not-expecting-life-to-get-any-better look, yet shining in from the back was something that made his heart warm…the glint of hope.

These kids needed all the hope they could get.

CHAPTER 15

"Wow." Jon stared at his picture. "That's awesome."

As if emboldened by Sean's picture, he turned and studied Robin. He took a deep breath and asked, "Why does your hair cover most of your face?"

Robin stared back at him. Why did his voice have to sound so much like her brother? His features were mobile with curiosity and childlike honesty. Given that, she told him the truth. "The one side of my face is badly scarred. My hair hides the scars."

His gaze locked on her face, studying the long fall of hair. She could almost see the wheels of his mind turning, figuring out, trying to imagine the damage and really wanting to ask her to show him, but not quite comfortable to take that step. Good thing. She was a long ways away from taking that step herself.

Hoping to stop him from gathering up the courage, she turned her attention to Sean. He was busy sketching. She marveled at the surety of his strokes, the absolute knowledge that his hand needed to place those marks where they needed to go.

Fascinating. She didn't have an artistic bone in her body. It was mesmerizing to watch it unfold in front of her. Sean had collected an assortment of observers from Jon to a little redhead boy with crutches to a set of twins wearing a series of leg braces. She had no idea what was going on with them, but they had a stoic look on their faces as if this wasn't anything new. And given the odd bend to their spines and legs, she suspected they'd had several corrective surgeries already with many more to come. It hurt her to realize what they were going through and likely not understanding how long and arduous the road ahead was going to be. Maybe that was a good thing.

"Daniel and David, give the man some room to work." A different nurse than they'd met last time walked toward them. She had a smile on her face but she was older, more reserved. She appeared to be okay with their presence, but she wasn't exactly rushing toward them enthusiastically.

She caught the woman's eyes, saw her gaze narrow speculatively, and Robin dropped her gaze to the floors. Adapting to the children was one thing. Adapting to curious adults was something else altogether.

But…she'd be damned if she'd keep hiding. She shoved a steel rod down her spine, straightened up, and stared back at the nurse. In the face of her own assertiveness, the nurse shifted her gaze away from Robin's face. Damn right.

Instead, the nurse nudged the twins back out of the way, not that they'd been in the way, and moved them toward the other end of the room. Robin let her gaze follow them, noting the fatigue in their arms, the droop to their shoulders by the time they made their way to their beds.

"Will you show me your face?"

Out of the blue, she felt like she'd been sideswiped by Jon's question.

Sean spoke up before she had a chance to answer. "It's not polite to ask something like that, Jon. If she wanted people to see it, she'd wear her hair differently so as not to hide it."

"I know…but…"

Sean, his voice firm, said, "No. Not right now. She'll let you see it only when she's ready."

"Scars are cool," Jon said.

"Some scars *are* cool. Some scars are tough."

Jon, his attention caught by the odd tone of Sean's voice, stared at him speculatively. "Do you have scars?"

"Sure." As if knowing what was coming, Robin watched Sean lift his hand off the paper and hold it out for Jon to see the shiny white marks along the back of his hand, the abnormally crooked fingers and thick knuckles.

"Neat." Jon studied them carefully. "Those don't look bad."

"Not now they don't. At the time, they were pretty ugly."

"What happened?" piped up Jon, his gaze never leaving Sean's hand.

"It's a long story. But the short version is one should never play with chicken wire."

Robin caught her breath. What could he have been doing with chicken wire to get marks like that? Or had he only said that to give Jon an answer he'd understand?

She glanced up to find Sean watching her, laughter in his eyes, inviting her to join in.

It was impossible to ignore it. She smiled back.

"You look like you're doing much better today."

She wrinkled up her nose at him. "The sky hasn't fallen down. The building hasn't collapsed. The children haven't run screaming…" She managed to swallow the word yet. "So far, so good."

SEAN STUDIED HER for a long moment, then he picked up his pencil and turned his attention back to the image he was creating. "Well, I'm proud of you."

She gave a half laugh. "Why, because I haven't bolted yet?"

"Actually – yes. That is a good sign. You also spoke to Jon. Who knows, maybe in a day or two you'll be comfortable enough to interact more with them."

"Maybe with Jon." She glanced around and realized thankfully that Jon had gone over to play with his friends. "It's easy to remember his name."

Sean, shading the shirt of one child, paused. There'd been a wash of emotion caught up in her voice.

"That accident that caused such damage to my face…"

He looked at her, saw the wet eyes, and waited.

"My baby brother was killed in that car accident. There was fifteen years between us. He'd have been close to Jon's age at the time he died. His name was also Jonathon."

"Ah hell." He put the pencil down and reached out to squeeze her shoulders gently. "I'm sorry, Robin. Did Jenna know?"

Robin flashed him a teary look and nodded.

"Of course she did."

Damn Jenna anyway. As if Robin didn't have enough to get over. An asshole boyfriend, multiple surgeries that took so much out of her she didn't care to have even one more. She'd travelled this road alone plus carried the survivor's guilt of being the only one left alive.

He dropped his hand and checked his watch. They'd been here an hour already. He wasn't going to have any pictures if he didn't get back to it. "I'm so sorry,"

She gave a brief nod but her head was still down and only her sniffles could be heard. She'd gone back inside.

Where no one else could go.

And that was starting to piss him off.

"Hey you," he said, his voice sharp, telling. "Stay out here. No more hiding."

"I wasn't trying to hide." She shrugged and the words burst out. "Why does he do this to me? He doesn't even look like Jonathon, but…there's something about him…"

"Sorry about that, but we have another hour and then it's time to go." He motioned to the kids around the room. "The reason we're here early is they have something else going on this afternoon. So this is almost over. Stay present."

"I am," she snapped, "I thought I was doing a fine job of it, too."

He grinned. "Much better." And it was. He'd rather have a female snapping at him than crying any time.

He watched approvingly as she straightened up and with her one good eye glared at him. "Wait. Don't move. Just stay like that."

Ignoring her snort, he flipped to a clean page and started sketching. She shifted slightly. He snapped out, "Don't move. No slumping. Stay straight and glare at me."

"That last part won't be hard," she said, aggravation in her tone, the set of her shoulders. "But I'm not a model. I can't just freeze in place."

"Try," he urged. "There's just something about the way you were sitting. It caught my eye."

His arm and hand moved at a desperate pace, trying to catch that elusive bit of imagery that he'd seen for a fraction of a moment.

There. Just as suddenly as he'd started, he stopped.

And stared.

"Let me see." Robin leaned forward to look and gasped. "Oh my!"

CHAPTER 16

ROBIN STARED AT the simple rendition of her sitting with her head slightly to the side and her nose upturned slightly. He'd captured her profile in what appeared to be just a few strokes. A few extra thin lines appeared to add shading. It was stunningly simple. Incredibly dramatic.

From the corner of her eye, she watched a slight tremor shake his hand that held the pencil. She let her gaze roam up his arm to where the edge of his t-shirt stopped. The t-shirt that hid the incredible damage to his shoulder. He might be a great artist, but he had physical difficulties in actually drawing.

No. She stopped considering it. He could draw, but not for long. If he drew on a regular basis, then the muscles would slowly build in strength and endurance. She hurt thinking about the ache he had to be experiencing. She sat back, her arm massaging her own shoulder. "It's very good. You're very good."

His lips quirked. "Thank you."

Yet his tone was dismissive. "No, I mean it." She reached out as if to touch her image but held back from making contact. "You really are talented." She looked up to study his face, noting the self-mockery. "You don't believe it, do you?"

He shrugged. "Sometimes I seem to be able to make something decent. Often I can't. I gave up out of sheer frustration. A lack of control is often the death of an artist, and sometimes," he shrugged and lowered his voice. "Sometimes my arm gives out completely."

She nodded. It was as she had suspected. "Still, it's something that you could strengthen and improve on."

His lips quirked. He tossed the pencil down. "If I cared enough."

"How could you not?" she exclaimed. "This," she wafted her hand toward the image, "is a gift."

"A common gift," he said, derision in his tone. "Many people draw."

"Not like you do." There was no way he could be lumped in with all the other artists in the world. He'd managed to capture the very essence of her – not just her, but the emotions coursing through her. The frozenness to her face, her smile on lockdown at all times. And the look in her eyes…that glare, but also what he'd pulled out from behind it.

She sat back studying that one aspect, then said in quiet tones, "You're very perceptive."

Silence.

"In what way?"

She made a strangled sound, took a deep breath, and said, "The fear in her eyes."

"Whose eyes?" he asked calmly.

Robin closed her eyes. After a long moment, she admitted, "*My* eyes."

He smiled at her gently.

"Am I really that obvious?" She turned to stare at him, almost hating him at that moment. "Is that what the kids see?"

He shook his head immediately. "No. Not at all."

"So what…you're just more perceptive than most people?" She glared at him, hating the anger coursing through her. And hating him for seeing that, too. Damn him. She got up and walked out of the ward.

SEAN WATCHED HER stride toward the double doors. Her pattern was still in effect. Run away to regain control then return when she could. He stared down at his picture, then turned to a clean page and with the last image he had of her in his mind, he quickly sketched her in the middle of her strategic retreat.

He didn't know why he felt the compulsion. She fascinated him. He'd seen compassion in her eyes when she looked at the kids, he'd seen pain in there too, but she'd managed to hold it back. Managed to keep that lid screwed down tight. It might be a glass lid that allowed others to see in and her to see out, but it was damn thick and secured in place.

What would happen if that glass broke?

The need to be normal drove her. Sent her to this workshop. Forced her to the hospital. No. He thought about that for a moment. She wanted to function normally. Only she'd never be normal.

She was too unique for that. Too special. Besides being normal was overrated.

Sensing sudden movement, he turned to see Robin already in her seat. His mind stopped for a second. She'd left, hadn't she? He blinked, trying to sort out what just happened.

She glared at him. Well, at least that was the same.

"I never left," she said by way of an explanation. "I kept

remembering your damn words."

He lifted his left eyebrow, not understanding.

"My pattern. You said I always run away then come back." Moodily, she stared around the room and the kids that likely hadn't noticed her even leaving. "I got to the door, even went so far as to push it open, and realized I was doing it again. You were right about my behavior pattern. And as doing the same thing over and over again keeps bringing me the same result over and over again, I have to change it. I want a new future. That means I need a new pattern."

"Or no pattern. All patterns eventually become a habit and a crutch." He should have kept his mouth shut. But instead of being upset or thinking he was being patronizing, she gave a gurgled laugh. "Well, there's no shortage of crutches here!"

CHAPTER 17

ROBIN SETTLED BACK, thinking about her old life –
before this week. She wondered just how bad it would
have gotten. Would she ever have left or found a way to
make her living without having to leave her home? She knew
that there was a name for people who couldn't leave their
homes, but she was damned if she could remember what it
was. She hadn't been that bad, but how long before she'd slid
all the way down?

"Thoughts?"

She winced. "I was actually thinking of how close I was
to becoming one of those housebound people."

"Ha. You're a long ways off from ending up like that."
He grinned, his pencil working on the paper. "You are here.
You are working on your problems. You're getting stronger
all the time."

"And you, what are your problems?" She sat back,
watching the mixed emotions slide across his face. Irritation.
Sadness. Denial. "Why exactly are you here? Or you aren't
going to tell me?"

"There's nothing to tell."

"Well, you don't appear to be learning anything about
yourself. Or being taxed emotionally in any way." She
frowned at the lack of expression on his face.

"What kind of reaction should I be showing?" He sat

forward, one eyebrow raised. "Tears? Sobs? Crying out in frustration or pain?"

"No, of course not." She stopped, confused. Just what had she expected? Maybe awkward silences? Going off on his own. Walking out in a temper.

"Truthfully…?" She shrugged. "I'm not sure."

"Well if and when it ever happens," his grin lit up the room, "then we'll both know."

She watched the look on his face. The humor masking the forced calm. The neutrality. The cold anger. And she knew a little more. "No, you wouldn't cause a scene. You'd get your back up and stare down anyone who'd dare hurt you. You'd never run away." She smiled gently. "You'd make sure they paid though. One way or another."

His eyebrows shot up. "You make me sound like an arrogant assassin bent on revenge."

"The image almost fits." She couldn't hold back the grin. "You're definitely assassin material."

He choked back a laugh. "Really?"

"Really."

Just then a commotion stirred up behind them. Robin turned at the foreign voice. "Excuse me, but we need to ask you to leave now."

"Oh right." Sean jumped to his feet. "Time ran away from us."

"Sorry," Robin said, standing up as well.

As she walked to the door, she heard a little voice behind her. "Are you leaving?"

She paused, her heart aching. Please don't let it be Jon. She was afraid to look into his face. See the lost look. The loneliness. She wanted to walk away. To pretend she hadn't heard him. Instead, her feet turned on their own will.

Jon stood in front of her. There was a thin detached look plastered on his face. She took a step back and smiled at him. Or at least she tried to smile. It wasn't successful. His features didn't change. There was still that faint hope, that desperation, that needing *something* from her. Something she didn't have to give.

"We have to go now." She leaned closer. "You have something else happening this afternoon."

Those fathomless eyes stared at her. Did he understand?

Sean tugged her arm. "Come on, we need to leave."

She looked at him pleadingly. He caught her gaze, and then turned to look at Jon. "Hey buddy. We'll be back tomorrow. Okay?"

The little boy stared up at him, that gaze not shifting. Then he nodded once.

SEAN LED ROBIN downstairs via the elevator and back outside, right into the pouring rain and across the parking lot to his truck. Just when he wondered if she was going to be okay, she separated and walked over to the passenger side of the truck and got in on her own. Progress. He watched while she buckled up and then locked her door. Good. She was much better today. Both about riding in a vehicle and about being here at the hospital. Maybe a couple more days would be enough for her to show real progress on the other issues. Although that little boy Jon was likely to be the end of her.

He reminded her of her little brother, had facial scarring similar to her own, and was in the middle of multiple surgeries. She could relate to him on a level Sean couldn't. But she refused to. She couldn't because she was stuck in her own pain. Her own mirrors.

She could do a lot for Jon.

Jon could do a lot for her.

But they both had to be able to meet somewhere in the middle for any of that to happen.

"What do you think happened to him?"

He didn't pretend to not know who she was talking about. "I don't know. Maybe you should ask him."

As soon as the words were out of his mouth, he wished he could bring them back. One rule he'd learned in hospital was to not ask too many questions. Some of the stories were easy, but many were tragic. It might help the child to share, but it didn't help those listening. Many had stories that hurt. And more often than not, it didn't take a newcomer long to realize there was always someone worse off than you.

"No, that would put him on the spot."

"Like asking you puts you on the spot?"

Silence.

He risked a glance her way. She was staring out the window, her face turned away from him. But there was that cold frozen profile again. Her face would be so mobile when she was with her friends or in the workshops. But with him, he was treated to the cold visage and lack of emotion.

"Why are you always so quiet around me?"

She turned to look at him. "I'm not."

"Sure you are. You spend more time being silent around me than you do talking to me."

She shrugged. "Up to now, you've been with me when I've gone through some difficult times."

Really? He snickered. "Nothing you've been through has been difficult. On the scale of what could have happened to you, this is all minor. It's time to get over you."

He hadn't meant to let that spew, but it was the truth

and therefore he didn't wish to retract the words and neither would he apologize. Paris had gone through so much worse than Robin and she'd never complained. He knew they were different people, and he thanked God he'd seen this moment today because it highlighted their differences in a big way.

Robin had the surgeries available. So many people didn't. She had a rough go of it. But there was a time to end that self-pity, too. So what if her face was disfigured? So what if she was sick of hospitals? Life was like that. Sure she'd lost her brother and the rest of her family and that just sucked. But this was too much "poor me" stuff. He wanted her to buck up and get over this mess.

"Wow."

He never said a word; he pulled the truck to a stop at the red light and glared out the window. "You live the life of the entitled," he snapped, "You have so much and all you can do is focus on the things you don't have."

"You mean like most people do."

"Maybe they do, but that doesn't mean they should."

"And what makes you so sure about what I should do?" she asked, but at least there was heat in her voice, anger in her tone.

"Good. Get mad. Feel something. Anything is better than always shutting down. That makes you…"

"A victim. Yes, I know," she said, her voice calmer but still strident. "But you don't need to speak to me that way; I do it enough for both of us."

"And there's that damn self-pity again. Whatever else is burning a hole in your gut, get it out and get over it. This is a slow painful death. And over what?"

He glared at her, his own temper building to the point he was likely to say more than he should. He'd probably already had. He revved the truck engine and hit the gas too hard, spinning the tires slightly on the wet pavement as the truck lurched forward. He watched her grab for her arm rest. And that just made him angry.

"You don't know what pain is. You don't know what rejection is." He snorted. "And for all your losses, you still haven't learned to roll with the punches."

She snarled in outrage, "What, so because I wasn't abused all my life, I don't have the right to feel my own anguish? I don't have the right to be upset because your life was so much worse than mine was? Is this a fucking contest?" Her voice rose to a high pitch at the end.

"Hell no." He half laughed. "If it were, you'd have lost a long time ago."

"That doesn't mean I'm not allowed to feel what I feel."

"Of course you can feel it. But feeling it and wallowing in it is not the same thing."

There was only silence for the rest of the trip. When they reached the hotel, she hopped out of the truck, slammed the door close, and ran inside ahead of him. He didn't know if that was to avoid him or to get out of the rain. That question was answered as she raced ahead to the wall of elevators. He followed close enough to see her step into the elevator, the door closing in his face.

He took the stairs three at a time, a dozen words boiling upwards. He came out onto the floor to see her walking to her room. No, not walking – running. She made it to her door, fumbled in her purse for her card, and finally managed to find it. She opened her door just in front of him, entering just as he reached her. She turned, saw him, and jumped back.

"What, did you come to gloat?" she said, tears spilling

down her cheeks.

"No," he said, hating the pain he'd caused. She'd needed to hear the words, but he wished he hadn't been the one to say them. He took a deep breath and broke his own long-time rule. "I came to apologize."

CHAPTER 18

APOLOGIZE? SHE WANTED to rip his head off. But his words broke the dam and instead of yelling at him, the tears flowed faster. He gave a muffled curse and suddenly she was tugged into his arms. She didn't want this. Not from him. But instead of pulling back, she was blubbering all over him. Worse yet, his comfort was working.

Damn.

She let the hot tears slow before finally stepping back to look up at him. "Sorry," she said, trying to speak in a normal voice and knew she'd failed when he snatched her back against his chest. A few straggling tears leaked. She sniffed a couple of times and tried to raise her hand to wipe her eyes, but her arms were pinned against his chest. A strong, whipcord-lean chest. Nice. She sighed. God, she was a mess. She should be slapping him silly for holding her like this, but all she could think about was that lean muscle beneath her hands…just waiting for her touch. Not that that was likely to happen. Too bad. She loved sex. Adored the sense of intimacy, of being part of a special twosome.

God, she missed that. And now that her libido had awakened…

She tugged her hand free and swiped at her cheeks. She must look a mess. "Excuse me," she muttered. His arms dropped away, letting her step back. She escaped into the bathroom. There, she stared at her ravaged face in the mirror. And damn if her tears didn't start to pour all over again. Still sniffling, she turned on the water and washed her face, hoping the cold water would help the puffy redness. She delayed as long as she could. What were the chances that he had left her alone?

If she'd read him right, none at all.

She didn't know where his harsh words came from, but he'd been right. Maybe not right to say such things to her, but he'd been right to have thought them. And she'd needed to hear them. As if the hospital visits weren't enough to remind her that her life could be so much worse.

When had it all become too much? She studied the left side of her face. When had she stopped planning for a better future? When had she really given up on the idea of finding love again? After the accident? Recently or somewhere in that long uphill climb in between.

Drained and thinking she'd somehow lost her way, she opened the door to find him still standing where she'd left him. She stopped just out of arm's reach. "Thank you."

He raised his eyebrows. "For being mean? For making you cry?" His voice hard and full of self-recrimination.

"No," she said gently, "For the reminder that life could be so much worse." She shrugged. "You were right. I was wallowing. It's an easy thing to do." She twisted her lips in a half smile. "As much as I don't like what you said, I needed to hear it."

She walked to the still open door and opened it wider. "You can leave now. I'm not going to do anything stupid." She was trying to give him a way out. He made no move to take it.

"Then as I said those truths, maybe you'll also listen

when I say *this* truth. You're a very beautiful woman."

She made a strangled sound, her hand already moving in a dismissive gesture when he reached out and caught her hand. "Stop. I've spoken the truth in all ways. Now listen."

She stilled. Her gaze locked on his face. Why would he say such a thing? As she searched his features, she realized another truth. He believed what he was saying. He was obviously blind but from his perspective, he believed she was beautiful.

Something inside loosened, warmed. She realized yet another bit of her icy shield around her heart had thawed again.

She sighed. And shook her head. "You need glasses."

"No, I don't." He smiled gently. "I can see you're working on your issues. That you are stuck on your exterior appearance. That you can't see the brave, valiant woman that I see. I'm sorry for that. Because if you could, you'd realize that you'd already accomplished so much this week, and it's not half over."

There was such a mix of emotions inside that she felt heavy, fatigued to the point of not being able to walk any further. Good thing she was already in her room. She slipped around him to sit on her bed. There was nothing intimate about the setting. Not like there could have been with having a man in her bedroom.

She rubbed her hand on her temple. "I'm trying to deal with my issues and failing miserably. I'm trying not to get hung up on my appearance, but that's a bit too big a step for me right now. All I see is the breakdown of who I am. The utter worthlessness inside. There are so many people worse off. I have nothing to complain about. See, you were right."

"Look, I'm sorry. I was harsh and cold. I knew you

needed to be smacked out of your self-pity, but I don't want you to take it so far that you can't see how well you're doing."

"I'm not doing well at all." She lay back on her bed. She just wanted to curl up into a ball and have the world go away. "Are you sure you're not a shrink?"

He laughed and sat down beside her. "No way."

But there was a tone to his voice. She looked over at him. "What?"

There was a slight hesitation, then he said, "Nothing."

It was her turn to frown at him. "What, so you can poke and prod at others but not share anything yourself?"

But the moment was gone. He shrugged and with a lopsided grin said, "Those that can…"

She reached out and slugged him.

SEAN LAUGHED. HE reached out and tugged her forward into his arms and gave her a hug. A real hug. A gentle, nonthreatening, hey-I'm-here-for-you type of hug. And was inexorably grateful when she didn't pull away. He'd been harsh on her. But it had worked and wonder of wonders, she appeared to have forgiven him.

"Let's go for dinner. Food will help settle the nerves."

She pulled back slightly. Her face was still punchy, but the smile was back in her eyes. "Thanks."

"Stop. Don't thank me. You are helping me as much as I'm helping you."

"Now if only I believed that." She studied his face carefully. "And the only way I could is if you'd explain."

He opened his mouth to push her off again and was surprised to hear the truth slide out. "I came for my sister's sake."

Robin tilted her head, her gaze narrowed thoughtfully. "Explain."

"Can we do this over a meal? I'm starved."

"As long as you do so." She grinned. "Although how you could be after that huge lunch, I don't know. Let's go."

They headed down to the restaurant and instinctively headed to the corner. Sean let her take her seat while he sat across from her. They barely had a chance to sit before the waitress was there with menus.

"I don't need a menu," he said and proceeded to order the house burger with fries. He waited as Robin smiled brightly up at waitress and said, "Make that two."

Damn, he liked that. A girl who could eat. And never whined about watching her weight or complaining about being on a diet. He'd seen Robin in a swimsuit and damn, but she was built. Nicely rounded yet slim and long lean limbs. Just the way he liked them.

After that, the waitress delivered water then coffee. By the time she'd left them alone, Sean realized Robin was itching for answers.

She leaned forward. "Well?"

He grinned. "Let me explain." And he proceeded to tell her about Paris trying to get into the workshop but being told to wait and asking him to attend for her.

Robin leaned back and stared at him. She slowly re-placed the cup of coffee she'd been holding. "Wow. That's a wonderfully weird thing to do."

That startled a laugh out of him. "I guess it's odd but as she asked…" He shrugged. "I love her. She's trying to heal, and if there is anything I can do to help her succeed in that direction, I'm willing to do it," he said simply.

He studied her glistening eyes in confusion. "Why are

you crying now?"

She sniffled several times but smiled though the tears. "It's a wonderful thing to do. I'm glad you care so much about her."

"She's had a tough life." He shrugged self-consciously, feeling exposed. He wasn't used to sharing his personal life. And never his personal feelings. Still, he owed Paris a debt he could never repay. "She was there for me all those years. There's not a lot I wouldn't do for her."

"I can't imagine what your childhood must have been like."

"We had no childhood," he said shortly, hating the sharp edge of anger rising up inside. The pain. The betrayal. No child should have to deal with what he and his sister had dealt with. No one person should – child or adult. Just as suddenly as it came, the anger sank back down.

"No, I imagine not." Robin took a sip of her coffee. "What does your sister do?"

"She's a nurse and works with children."

That brought Robin's eyebrows up. "Like where we were today?"

"Sort of, but not quite." He shook his head. "She works in the maternity ward."

"Good for her. I'm not sure I could do that job."

"She's a gentle soul." He smiled. "And she loves babies."

"Sounds like she should have a dozen of her own."

"That won't ever happen." He couldn't help it. His voice hardened as the memories piled into his brain and plugged up his thinking. Paris's abuse had been different than his but just as violent. Just as insidious and just as permanent.

Robin gasped in sympathy. "I'm so sorry for her. It's one thing to not be able to have children if that's not something you particularly cared to do, but if it is…" She winced then added, "I can't imagine anything worse."

Sean nodded. "She struggles with it sometimes. She loves to see the happy mothers, the beloved children. Every once in a while it's tough on her. Particularly when she has mothers in having their third and fourth and not wanting to be having the child. Stuck by circumstances or timing or just not caring enough to do something about not getting pregnant. And all she can do is help the woman through the process. Sometimes they are very voluble about their dislike of the whole process and in particular the child."

"Oh no." Robin shook her head. "It's a terrible thing in today's world to think of such a problem. Every child deserves to have a loving home and adoring parents. At least one parent."

"I feel the same way," Sean said. "Then again, I don't plan to have any kids, so it's not a big deal for me."

He stared out the window, feeling the intensity of Robin's gaze heat up. There was no way to explain that he was afraid he had more of his father in him that he suspected. That he'd rather kill himself than hurt a child like he'd been hurt. That he'd never want to be the kind of father like his own and that genetically it was all too possible. The pain had to stop somewhere, and he'd chosen to make sure it stopped with him.

"Maybe Paris will be able to adopt a half dozen, and then you'll have lots of nieces and nephews to practice your parenting skills on," Robin said lightly.

"No practice required. But I do think I'd enjoy being an uncle."

At that moment their food arrived, breaking the conversation at a great place. Sean tucked in.

CHAPTER 19

Robin's shoulders and back were knotted again. She rotated her shoulders and winced. Between the stress and fears, she'd locked her muscles, and they'd retaliated by staying locked. She was going to have to go to the pool and hot tub again. She'd left Sean outside in the hallway. He'd looked as if he wanted to say something to her. Do something. Invite her somewhere. She'd needed to be alone.

Only now that she was alone...she didn't want to be.

She'd checked her emails and studied her notes for tomorrow, thinking to get ahead on the assignments, only to find her mind unable to focus.

Now she had to wonder if her real wish to go to the pool had more to do with the possibility that Sean might go there as well. Or he could be sitting in the bar. She tossed that suggestion aside. She didn't think he was a drinker. Not a heavy one anyway. That would mean it was all right to lose control. She highly suspected control was important to him.

He'd held her with that same careful control. She couldn't believe how much she missed being held by a man. One who cared? Sean didn't care about her more than what they were to each other through this course... but she was starting to realize she wanted him to. Would he want to stay in touch after this week was over? She pondered that question while she got changed into her bathing suit. She had no idea where in the lower mainland he lived. She thought everyone in the workshop attended UBC, but she hadn't seen anything to indicate that Sean was a student.

He also wasn't here for himself.

She had mixed feelings about that. It was like he wasn't supposed to be here. Wasn't *trying* to heal like the rest of them. She'd have tacked on that he wasn't as broken as the others in the workshop, but she was realizing that in many ways, he was likely worse. Those in the workshop were at least admitting that they had problems and were willing to work on them. Not only willing but eager. Sean, by contrast, hadn't acknowledged he had a problem. At least not to her.

Although he'd been very good with the children. And how he could be, she didn't know. Given what he'd shared about his childhood, she had to wonder at the scars. He had many outside, but there were just as many on the inside.

How could there not be?

Still, he was remarkably normal.

Because of his sister.

There'd been love and support between them. A bond she imagined had been forged in hell. A bond that had kept them alive. Kept them sane. They'd both survived and thrived as well as they could, but they'd also hit that point where they couldn't do much more on their own. They needed help. Paris knew it. She'd been looking to come to the workshop. Robin could only imagine her disappointment.

From what little Sean had shared about her, Robin felt a kinship. She'd love to meet her. She couldn't remember ever seeing her at the evening sessions. Then again, she hadn't seen Sean there either. Although lately Robin had been missing more classes as it became harder to force herself out of her home. That tiny space had become an all-too-comfortable jail cell.

Crap. Unsettled and determined to stay in the progressive path, she snagged her housecoat off the bathroom hook and let herself out of the hotel room. She took the stairs to the pool deck and quickly stashed her belongings in a cubicle. There were several people in the pool and the hot tub appeared full. That was fine. She needed to work her poor muscles. Physio had helped all those years, but she needed to keep up the exercises. Something she often forgot.

Walking to the end of an empty lane, she curled her toes and dove in. The water was refreshing and cool. She struck out strongly and lost herself in the rhythmic pull of the muscles.

The car accident had left her with more than obvious scarring. The damage to her right leg, hip, and shoulder were likely to bother her most of her life. She'd taken the impact directly. She'd been leaning over her young brother when the collision happened and her hip had taken the worse of it, but the force had thrown her forward and sideways. It was the shards of glass and the multiple shattered bones and lacerations that had done the most obvious damage.

She remembered lying in the vehicle hearing the rescuers talk about the deceased in the accident. She'd thought they'd been talking about her. It hadn't been until she'd woken up in the hospital and found out that everyone else had died except for her.

It sucked to be the only survivor.

SEAN WATCHED AS Robin strode up to the edge of the pool in her typical straightforward attitude. She gripped the edge of the pool with her toes, her long muscles flexing, and she dove off in perfect form. She'd had lessons somewhere along the line. Lucky girl. He rarely thought of all that he'd missed out on in his childhood, but the differences between those normal families and his showed up at the oddest times. Like now.

She was a stunner even with the tight skin and the shiny look to her face. He could just imagine how far she'd come if the accident had been as bad as he suspected. Her shoulder had been injured and he doubted she was aware of it, but she walked with a limp when she was tired. In the morning, no one would notice. By the end of the day, she slowed down and it became more pronounced.

He thought of a bad accident with her in the back seat getting hit – if the impact had been on her side of the vehicle, it would explain the limp on her right side. He imagined her hips and possibly her ribs had taken the brunt of the hit. He winced just thinking about it. One minute you're talking and laughing and then smash...you were hit broadside and there was no more laughter in your world.

He knew she felt guilty. That she'd lost her younger brother had to be tough, but to lose *all* her family at the same time...wow. Considering everything, she'd been a trooper at the hospital. Not that he was ready to tell her that. He hoped she was ready to let her hair down – or rather put her hair up so she'd be who she really was to those kids. He doubted any of them would run screaming from her.

Between the kids in that ward, there were some major injuries and a lot of reconstructive surgery going on. They were – in the words of boys everywhere – 'awesome' looking injuries. He grinned, remembering the few times some of the other school kids had seen his injuries. They'd been jealous.

It had made it easier to live through the experience. He and Paris used to play a game trying to determine the length of time for their bruises to change color. Sometimes they never had a chance to know because fresh ones were laid on top of the old.

He looked back down the empty lane where he'd been doing laps. He'd wanted to ask Robin to come up to the pool area with him but had sensed her refusal. He was used to that. Now he'd ended up here with her anyway. Sounded good to him. He just had to maneuver the two of them alone together again.

Long and lean and strong on the inside. She might not agree with that assessment, but then again, she didn't see herself the way he did.

He did another lap and felt his shoulder struggle to pull its weight. He'd been at it for long enough. Every day it seemed to get better, but if he dared miss a day or two, it was as if all progress was lost and he was back to the beginning. He used the pools at the university a lot. He wondered why he hadn't seen more of Robin.

With both of them being on campus, their paths had to cross sometimes…

UBC was a huge campus, almost a city in itself, with so many paths and buildings and different routes to travel that there was no need for two people to meet if they didn't want to, but as they both attended Jenna's evening lectures…

It was too bad they hadn't met before – several times even. If they had, they'd be much further along this path right now. And he had no doubt where that path was going. Except he felt different about her. He didn't want the same thing. Hell, that was a lie…he did want the same thing…he just wanted more. So much more. Paris would be delighted.

He wasn't so sure. He hated this uncomfortable feeling. This sense of always looking to see where she was. What she was doing. Always thinking about her. Worrying…

Christ. This sucked. He was a long ways away from taking her into his arms and loving her the way he wanted to make love to her. Those scars she was so worried about were meaningless to him.

In all ways.

Now if only he had the chance to prove it to her.

CHAPTER 20

ROBIN STOPPED WHEN she couldn't lift her arm for one more stroke. Maybe that had knocked her libido back down to reasonable levels again. She was hot, but it was from exertion and not sexual tension. She hoped. She didn't want to see Sean and put it to the test.

Breathing deep, she pulled herself up to sit on the edge of the pool until her breathing calmed down. She lifted her arms and wiped the water from her eyes. Normally she swam with goggles, but she'd forgotten hers at home in the fear and excitement of packing for the workshop. Swimming goggles had hardly been a priority. Blinking several times, she turned to look around. The pool had emptied and there were a couple of people left in the hot tub. It looked too damn far away to bother. But her body throbbed with pain.

And the hot water would help. She brushed her hair forward to hide her face before clambering to her feet. It was only as she stood swaying in place that she realized how tired she really was. By the time she made her way to the hot tub, she was ready to collapse. And damn, that hot water was going to suck the last of her energy away. Getting back to her hotel room was going to be a bitch.

She stood at the edge of the hot tub contemplating her options.

"Robin? Are you okay?"

Sean. She glanced down at him. Of course he'd be here. Why couldn't it be Tania? She'd barely seen her friend thus far at the conference.

She gave Sean a wan smile. "I'm okay. I think I just overdid the swimming part. Now I'm afraid the hot water will finish me and I won't be able to get back to my room."

He stood and reached up to gently grasp her elbow and helped her into the hot water. "The water will help the sore muscles, and I'll help you get to bed."

She almost laughed at his wording. Before her accident, she'd have teased him about the double entendre. In this case, it was likely accidental. Too bad. She wished he would help her to bed – his bed.

Groaning at the warmth as she sank into the water, she closed her eyes and dropped her head back on the edge. "This feels so good," she murmured.

"Yeah, it does."

Because they weren't alone, he sat down beside her. Keeping her voice low, she asked, "How's the arm after today's session?"

He opened and flexed his right hand a couple of times. "Better."

She snorted. "Not likely."

"What?" He grinned. "You think you know me now?"

"Oh, I know you." She smirked. "The good and the bad."

There was a stilted silence. She rolled her head in his direction and smiled at him. "What? Did I say something wrong?"

He shook his head. "I was just thinking how few people really know me. Paris is the only one."

"And now me."

There was a tiny sound followed by something that sounded like *I wish*. But he'd spoken so low she wasn't sure. Going on instinct and hating to think of him so alone, she reached over and covered his hand with hers.

Immediately, under cover of the foamy bubbles, he closed his fingers over hers.

Her heart thumped and she smiled on the inside. She leaned her head back and for the first time all day, she just relaxed. The heat soaked deep into her muscles, letting the damaged and recovering tissue ease back their tightness, which in turn helped them to relax.

A few minutes later, she groaned softly. "This was the right decision."

"Definitely."

There was a teasing note to his voice. She grinned and opened her eyes to see they were alone in the hot tub. She twisted to search the rest of the large room and found to her surprise that the big room was completely empty.

"Wow, where did everyone go?" She settled back into the water and let her body float upward in the water. She loved doing this, but normally the hot tubs were too full of other people. She let go of Sean's hand and stretched out completely. "Hope you don't mind," she said with a laugh.

"Go for it."

She leaned her head back and floated, letting the water bubble up around her. God, it felt good. "Too bad it's not big enough for two of us to do this."

The next thing she knew, Sean had stretched out on the surface of the water, gently bumping up beside her. She laughed.

The world, for all the troubles of the last few days, seemed ideal right now.

"This is perfect," she said, her eyes drifting close but her smile still firmly in place. "I'm really glad I came tonight."

"Almost perfect," he said, "but there is one place I'd like to see you in even more."

Her eyes flew open, her head rolling slightly to face him. "Oh, where's that?"

She was gently turned and then shifted so she was upright, the water churning around her waist. While she was still adjusting to her change in position, he tugged her into his arms and said, "Right here."

And he lowered his head and kissed her.

AS FAR AS impulsive actions went, it was one of the best he'd taken in a long time.

The cool chill of her lips hid a banked heat that he couldn't get enough of. He wondered if he ever would. She had the sweetest, softest lips. He coaxed them to open for him. Her response was tentative at first, then she seemed to get over the shock and she became downright enthusiastic. And that was all he needed. His hands slid down her wet back to cup her rounded buttocks and pulled her tight against him. She wiggled closer.

He groaned.

She moaned.

He crushed his lips against hers before a heavy shudder wracked his frame. He eased back and slipped his tongue inside to duel with hers. Regardless of her initial response, she was there with him all the way now.

And damn him for starting this in a public place.

He wished they were standing in her bedroom where he could take this further. Take her to bed like he wanted to. A thought never far from his mind lately. Foolish. He wasn't here for this. He hadn't come looking for this.

Neither was he going to turn this down.

He was a healthy male. She was a dynamite sexy woman who'd lost her self-confidence. If nothing else, he could help her with that. She was still that same person – only now she was so much more.

She needed to remember that.

To learn that deep inside.

To take it in and own it.

He hadn't learned his lessons easily. Three days ago, he'd have told anyone that he hadn't learned any lessons. That he'd had no lessons to learn. In his arrogance. In his disdain of his fellow man. In his need to stay separate and detached from everyone around him, so as to not get hurt.

Then Robin happened. She'd shown him just how far he'd come – and just how far he had yet to go. He had no experience with long-term relationships. The last thing he wanted from her was a one-night stand. That left him uncertain, nervous as to how to proceed. Before, he hadn't cared if things worked out with a woman. Now he didn't want to screw up.

On that note, he pulled back and tugged Robin against his chest, her head tucked under his chin.

He held her close. He held her against his heart.

Just where she belonged.

CHAPTER 21

ROBIN SHOOK SO hard she needed to lean against him for support. For a first kiss, that was unbelievable. Talk about mind blowing. And all she could think about was another one. Heat fired through her at the thought. God, if she had this type of response to his kiss, what would making love be like? She whimpered then caught her breath, hoping he hadn't heard her. But he dropped a tender kiss on her forehead, then another on her temple. She tilted her head back, giving him better access if he wanted it.

He lowered his head and dropped a gentle kiss on her lips.

"We're going to need to take this up somewhere private or be prepared to be interrupted here."

She stiffened, jerked back, and hurriedly looked around. "Dear God, are we alone?"

A warm deep laugh rumbled up from his chest. "We are. At the moment."

"Jesus." She sank back into the water and dropped her face in, letting the foam rush up and over her features. She couldn't believe she'd forgotten where she was. She sat up, brushing her hair back off her face. She didn't know what to do – how to proceed. She took a deep breath. "I think I'll go up to my room."

He helped her out of the hot water before walking ahead

of her to pick up her robe and wrap it around her. "Come on. I'll help you back up."

"What about your robe? Did you not have one?"

He laughed. "I didn't bring one. I just came down in my shorts and..." He stopped and looked around the space. "And...my t-shirt." He walked over several feet and picked up a green shirt she hadn't noticed until now lying on the tiles. As she watched, he tugged it over his head then turned to her and held out his hand. "Come on."

It felt momentous. A turning point.

It also felt...right.

HE ESCORTED HER, damp footsteps tracking behind them on the hotel carpet, to the back elevators. Within minutes they'd reached their floor. He led her to her room and waited for her to pull her card out of her robe's pocket and unlock the door.

So far, she'd said nothing. Had given no sign of her intentions.

His stomach knotted. He wanted her with him tonight. And tomorrow. God, he had it bad. And he hadn't had any warning. He hadn't seen it coming. It had blindsided him. From one moment to the next.

No, that wasn't quite true. She'd crept up on him slowly, gaining a little more inroad to his heart every hour, every day. What the hell did that make him? Besides a fool. All of it pissed him off. The uncertainty. Not knowing his next step. What to say. How to act.

With the door pushed open, Robin stepped inside and turned to face him.

His frustration waned. Expectation rose. He wanted to

close his eyes – therefore he stared right at her. And waited for her say something.

Sex was straightforward. He didn't know how to handle relationships. No idea how to start one. He'd never had to. Or even to understand if they had the start of one. God, he hoped so. He didn't think he could trust himself to make these types of decisions if he was wrong this time.

He couldn't be wrong. *This* couldn't be wrong. It felt too right.

She smiled, reached up, and kissed him gently. "Thank you."

"Ask me in." The words blurted out of his mouth with all the subtlety of a green teenager.

"Do you think it's wise?"

"Ask me in," he repeated, hating the tiny plea that entered his voice, hoping she didn't hear it. When she studied him…and never said a word, he couldn't bear it and he added one thing – one thing he'd thought to never say in this situation. "Please."

CHAPTER 22

O H LORD. SHE'D been all set to refuse him – her mind at
odds with her jumping jack hormones. Then he'd said
please…and that final layer of frost around her heart started
a downward slide.

She pushed the door open wider.

His gaze widened. He glanced from the door to her, and
when she didn't move, his eyebrow rose and his lips quirked.
"Is that an invitation or only half an invitation?"

She gave him a slow easy smile. "I guess it doesn't matter – both say yes."

He entered and closed the door behind him. The shadows fell across his cheekbones, his forehead giving him a
fallen angel look. She hadn't turned a light on, and now she
was glad. The darkness was a blessing. It hid so much. And
showed much more.

Snick went the lock. He turned to face her, his gaze
heavy lidded, his eyes almost black with emotion, and
opened his arms.

He was even now giving her a choice.

She didn't want one. She needed this. She was grateful
that he didn't appear to be put off by her disfigurement. She
had no trouble with his scars either. She'd suspected sex with
Sean would be a wild ride. And damn it, she wanted to strap
in and enjoy.

And yet she hesitated.

It had all gone by so fast. She barely knew Sean. No, her mind rejected that. Sean no longer qualified as a stranger. She might not know all the details about his life, but she knew the person that stood before her – probably as well as she had any man. Then again, she'd have sworn that her boyfriend, Tom, could never have said the things he'd said.

Comparing Sean to Tom was wrong. They were nothing alike. Sean was the antithesis of Tom. Sean was…complicated. Yet he had an honor system and a code. They might be difficult to live by, but she'd take that over superficial any day.

She smiled up at him.

He opened his mouth, and in a gentle tone, asked, "Second thoughts?"

"No," she said. "I was just thinking how much I prefer deep, dark, and broody to shallow and superficial."

His eyebrows shot up and he stared at her, his head tilted slightly to the side. He was confused. Good. It would serve him right. He'd kept her off balance more than she cared to admit. Before he could formulate the question that was working through his psyche, she stepped into his arms.

She reached up and tugged his head down and kissed him.

As his arms closed around her, more comforting than lover-like, and his lips were warm but not hot, she quirked her own lips slightly. He was still giving her a chance to back away.

She pulled back slightly and dropped her robe to the floor. Now she stood in her wet bathing suit. She stepped back one more step, deeper into the shadows. She slipped the straps off her shoulders and lowered the clinging material to her waist. She watched him as he watched her.

There was no way he could see the details, but she knew what the shadows would highlight.

When he gasped slightly, a flush rising slightly across his cheeks, she grinned inside. Good. In a hard tug, she had the bathing suit pooling on the floor. She gave the material a kick and sent it flying across the room and stood before him. Nude. Scarred. Ready.

"Second thoughts?" she asked, repeating his earlier words, motioning to his modest attire. "And just so it's a non-issue. I'm on the pill to regulate my cycle." She wrinkled up her nose at him. "The drugs from the surgeries messed things up big time."

He galvanized into action so fast she laughed. But her laughter was choked off a few seconds later as she was picked up, swung into a wide circle, then tossed on the big bed.

And he came down on top of her.

"You are amazing," Sean said, before he covered her mouth with his.

As long as he thought so, she'd let him live the dream a little longer. Even join him in it for a little while. At least as long as she was in his arms.

Then she couldn't think as his kisses turned her insides to mush. Still damp from their wet bathing suits, their bodies steamed as legs tangled with legs and hands caressed and stroked what each could reach as they both gave and took in equal measures.

She realized dimly, somewhere in the back of her mind, that he was good at this. Like he was seriously good at this. He was so caring, attentive, appreciative. He made her feel special. How sexy was that?

She realized, as his lips teased a hot blazing trail of kisses downward to one breast, a breast with some scar tissue marring the perfect flesh, that she was the richer one in this situation. She'd loved and had been loved. She knew what it was like to wake up beside someone you cared about in the morning. To feel blessed they were in your life.

She could show him some of that.

Except he was frying her circuits, making it so she couldn't think. He took her nipple deep into his mouth and suckled. She reared up, gasping with joy and frustration. God, she wanted him. Like now. Like hot and ready and inside her now.

"Sean," she cried out, twisting beneath him.

"Easy, sweetheart, take it easy."

"No," she cried out, her hands tugging on him. "Not easy. Now."

When he refused to slide up higher, she shifted downward and rolled him over. He laughed and flipped onto his back, tugging her over and with him.

"Patience," he murmured, pulling her down to his mouth and kissing her with one of his heavy, drugging kisses that she craved.

"No patience," she gasped against his lips when she could. "Next time. We'll take it slow and easy then."

She planted a knee on either side of his hips, slipped down his body until she felt him, rigid, hard, hot at her center. She sat up and lowered herself slowly, oh so slowly, until he was seated deep inside. Watching his eyes cloud with passion was a turn on like no other.

Sean groaned, his eyes slowly closing, his fingers clenching her hips, holding her in place as he ground his pelvis upwards.

She shuddered, already so close to the edge.

"Jesus, you'll be the death of me," he whispered in a husky voice.

"Not yet, but soon," she murmured, her eyes closed. She started to ride. Initially she set a slow languid pace, reveling in the sense of fullness, the perfect fit of the two of them, the hard leanness of his body, but Sean urged her on, faster and faster. She leaned forward to brace her hands on his chest, holding her rhythm. Sean held her hips back from going too high.

She cried out, "Sean…"

"I'm here," he whispered. "Faster…

"I can't…" She tried to go faster, but her urgency and drive sent her rhythm off. Frustrated, he did a quick flip, startling a cry out of her, as their positions reversed. He lifted her leg over his arm and plunged deep.

She shrieked, her back arching as tiny explosions started deep inside. Then she came apart.

With a heavy guttural groan, he followed her.

SEAN ROLLED TO the side, completely wiped. He groaned lightly and tugged her into his arms. "I'm wasted. You completely wore me out."

She sniggered, the cheeky sound bringing a smile to his face.

"If you're worn out that easily, you'll be comatose by morning."

He shouted with laughter and kissed her again. She responded with all the enthusiasm as she had the first time. God, he loved that about her. The honesty of her reaction. The responsiveness of her passion. The clarity of her need. He needed that.

He needed her.

He was starting to think he'd need her forever.

Shuddering with the emotions swamping him, he pulled back to stare down at her. And realized he'd not taken the time to look at her. To *really* look at her. The room was dark. And he wanted to see her in the light.

The shadows earlier had hid her beauty.

He reached for the lamp switch.

"Don't." Her voice was harsh, clear. She cleared her throat. "Please."

He let his arm drop, not sure what to say yet hating that she didn't want him to see her like this. And not sure what to do about it.

He tugged her into his arms, his cheek against hers, and just held her.

After a long moment, he pulled back slightly and looked her straight in the eyes. He watched her gaze widen with worry. He smiled reassuringly. "It's all right. If you don't want a light, that's okay."

She searched his gaze and he let her see the acceptance in his eyes. The acceptance in his heart. He understood. More than most.

"Thank you," she whispered.

"You're welcome." He dropped a kiss on her nose. Then her cheeks. He pushed her hair back so he could look at the scarred side of her face closer. He hadn't done that yet. Hadn't had a chance to. He hadn't wanted to push. Now it wasn't pushing. It was time for rejoicing. Well, maybe not. She wasn't there yet. But he could help her take one more step toward it.

He kissed the spot where the tight skin pulled the corner of her mouth up and back. Bright pink skin, no longer angry, but quite normal looking – *if* it would ever become normal. It may not. He was fine with that. She was beautiful to him. Beautiful inside and out.

Somehow he had to make her see that. He grasped her face and held it firmly so she couldn't pull away while he kissed every inch of the shiny skin. Worshipped the misshapen skin and the rough edges where the scars joined the smooth healthy skin. She wouldn't need much more to make this all perfect looking, but he did understand how imperfect something in progress looked. He had been there. Was still there.

Yet his scars didn't appear to bother her.

So he needed to make sure she knew that her scars didn't bother him.

He followed the line of her neck down to her shoulder blades where there were more scars. More spots where her skin was marred from its creamy perfection. But not taking away from it. In fact, as he pulled back to stare at the pink skin, it added to it. She was beautiful.

And she misunderstood his actions. She slapped her hand across her shoulder, hiding. "Don't look," she whispered. "Turn away."

"Never," he whispered and showed her how much he cared about her. How much he adored her. How much he worshipped her. Her perfect body. How all the spots she hated only added to her beauty. To her uniqueness. She was stunning in her passion.

They had hours ahead of them. He planned to make sure she knew that by morning. That she knew he adored her. Every inch of her.

He smiled as he looked down at her and whispered under his breath, "But I'm up for the job."

She looked up at him, a puzzled frown on her face. "What did you say?"

"How about I show you instead…"

And he lowered his head.

CHAPTER 23

MORNING BROKE SLOW and hazy for Robin. Within minutes, she realized something else. She wasn't alone.

Memories flooded in. Last night. Sean – all night. Oh God.

What a night. Considering she'd gotten no sleep, she had no right to feel as rested as she did. She felt energized. Invigorated. As if she had a whole new day in front of her. She reached up and rubbed her face with both hands.

And stilled. Her hand gently stroked the scars on her face. Maybe not a *new* day. Still, it was a different day. Different from yesterday at least. That she'd take.

She looked over to see Sean stretched out dead to the world in the center of the bed. Her back was tucked up against him. She smiled. She might feel on top of the world, but he looked dead to the world. She wanted to giggle and shout for joy but held back. He needed what little rest he could find. She'd just slip out and grab a shower. Then wake him up.

It was early yet. They had a little time before going down for breakfast. Thank heavens, she thought as she stared into the bathroom mirror. She was going to need every bit of that time to make herself presentable.

She stepped into the shower and let the hot water sluice

down over her body. She wanted to keep his scent on her, but they'd made love so many times, she was afraid that it would be obvious to anyone who walked past her. This night had been special. Important. And she didn't want to share it with anyone.

She wanted to keep it between just her and him.

They hadn't spoken of love. Of tomorrow. Of togetherness. In fact, they'd barely spoken at all.

The water splashed into her face and she laughed, loving it. The spray both stung and soothed at the same time. She stood, face forward, grinning like a madman.

And realized time was running down the drain along with the water while she'd been standing there like a fool. She finished, then turned off the water and toweled dry.

She brushed her hair into her normal style, covering her face. She stared her face for a long moment, wondering if it was time to change but realized that she wasn't ready for that much change.

Gathering up her towel, she walked back into the bedroom and quietly got dressed. When she was done, she sat down on the side of the bed, stared at the masculine feast in front of her with regret, and woke him. "Sean?"

His eyes flew open and he stared at her. And heat kindled deep inside. "Good morning," he said in a gruff voice. He tugged her down to sprawl across his chest and gave her a deep morning-after kiss.

She was flustered by the time she managed to pull back. "It's late. We don't have time for any more of that."

"Ha." He gave her a lazy grin. "We could miss the workshop. Spend the day in bed."

"Oh boy," she muttered half under her breath, unbearably torn. Memories of the night swamped her body with remembered heat. She wanted that again. And again.

"As tempting as that is, I do need to complete the workshop." She smiled regretfully down into those languid eyes and sighed. "I really want to stay here but…"

"But you want to go the workshop more." He tugged her back down, kissed her hard, and then set her back in place. "Right then. I need to shower and find some clothes." He looked around, gathered up his clothes, and snatched up her robe, a question in his eyes. When she nodded, he put it on and slipped out of her hotel room. She followed him to the doorway and watched as he slipped inside his room. The door closed quietly behind him.

He hadn't said a word about how long he'd be, so she wasn't sure what she should do. Wait for him? Go into his room and wait for him? Or head down to the restaurant and wait for him there?

She should have asked. Oh well, it was too late now, he was likely already in the shower and wouldn't hear her knock. She headed back inside and packed up her notes for the morning session and cleaned up her bathing suit still sitting on the floor. She hung it up, a silly grin on her face. Would she ever see it again and not smile from the memory?

After hooking her housekeeping tag on her door, she walked down to the elevators and clicked the button. She'd wait for him down at the restaurant. As the elevator doors opened, she walked out into a small crowd. It was a popular hotel. There looked to be a large group checking out, even though it was still early. She slipped around them and came face to face with Jenna.

Jenna's face beamed. "Hi Robin, you're looking particularly bright today."

Robin managed a sheepish grin in spite of the heat washing up her neck. "Thank you. It's amazing what a good night's sleep will do for you."

"I'm glad to hear that. If your sleep is improving, that means you are healing on some level."

That made sense. She was healing. She could thank Sean for that.

Not wanting to share the details of the healing process with Jenna, Robin walked past with a murmur, "I need to get some breakfast."

Jenna nodded, a pleased smile on her face. "You don't have much time, but you can grab something to go."

Lord, she hoped they weren't that late. She checked the clock on the restaurant wall as she entered. Ugh. It was after 8:30. She really didn't have much time. And Sean had even less. She took a seat up at the front and ordered toast to eat now and several muffins to go. She gulped down a cup of coffee drenched in cream and ordered two more to go. After scoffing down her toast and wondering at her appetite, she gathered up her purchases and carried them over to the seminar room. It was already full. Tania was sitting in some kind of cold truce with Kane. The workshop was half over – at least she thought it was, she'd lost track of time. Was it Wednesday or Thursday today?

After a quick glance around, she realized Sean still wasn't there. She took a seat where there were two empty spots and sat down. She immediately went to work on the first muffin. Lord, she was still hungry. If Sean didn't get here soon, she was going to eat his two as well.

Just then, the chair beside her was pulled out and Sean sat down.

He reached for a coffee, assessed the muffin situation, and grabbed up two for himself.

She kept her head down in case her smirk alerted the others to the change in their relationship. She didn't care. Her body glowed and her heart sang. She had no illusions that this was a relationship. By his own admittance, he didn't know what one was. But she was grateful for what they did have. She hadn't felt this alive in months.

Quite possibly years.

AFTER A LATE arrival for the seminar and a crazy busy morning working on Jenna's assignments, before Sean realized it, they were breaking for lunch. He rose from his chair when Jenna called them over.

"Sorry you two, but this afternoon at the hospital is out," Jenna said. "You'll need to work on your project here at the hotel. It's possible you might be able to go later this evening, otherwise it will have to be tomorrow morning. I'm hoping that after two days there you have enough to get some serious effort done on the project just in case your time is shortened even more."

She turned to walk away when Sean stopped her. "Why? What's going on?"

"One of the kids has taken a turn for the worst. The other kids are having a tough day."

"Maybe we should go today especially for that reason," Sean said. He was afraid he knew which boy had taken a bad turn. Figured that Robin, from the frozen look on her face, had jumped to the same conclusion, too. She shuddered. A visible shake of her shoulders that must have gone straight to her toes. Shit. She didn't need this. Hell, neither did he. He'd had high hopes for more private time. At Jenna's initial words, he'd wanted to shout for joy. Now he knew that a private afternoon in bed with Robin wasn't going to be.

"No. The department head has requested that not happen. The children want their privacy while they deal with their emotions." She studied Robin's features even as Sean studied Jenna's.

"It's Jon, isn't it?"

Jenna's face became a polite mask. "Who?"

"A little boy that looked so very much like my brother."

Jenna's face became a mask of concern. "I'm sorry if that is the case. He's still alive though, so we have to hope."

"I want to go see him."

"No." Sean and Jenna both shouted.

Robin squared her shoulders. "Yes. I need to. Don't you see? I've associated him with my brother. I couldn't help it. There were so many similarities. Now that he's in trouble, I want to be able to do what I couldn't do before."

Jenna walked closer, her hands reaching out to grasp Robin's. "You don't know this boy. You aren't family. You can't go in and see him."

Robin's eyes glistened. Sean felt his heart sink.

"I have to go say goodbye," Robin whispered. "I have to."

She broke free of Jenna's hands and turned, running from the room.

"Damn it." Sean glared at Jenna. "See what happens when you meddle in other people's lives?"

She gave him a sad smile. "It's what I do. Before there can be healing, one must let go of the blockages. In this case, Robin has never fully grieved for her family. She can't go forward until she finally lets go of the past."

Sean knew she was right but hated hearing it. He didn't want Robin to suffer, and she was going to do plenty of that before this day was over.

He started after Robin.

"Sean." Jenna called out.

He turned but didn't walk closer. "What?"

"What are you going to do?" she asked, her gaze a pool of compassion. She might meddle in other people's lives, but she didn't do it lightly. Every time one of her students hurt, Sean realized Jenna did, too.

He said quietly, "Talk her out of it, or take her there myself."

She stilled, her gaze intent. "Why?"

He looked to see if she was serious. Realizing she was, he shook his head and said, "Because that's what friends do."

And he walked away, wondering at her last question. Then made a startling realization. He had no idea what friends did.

Because he'd never had one before.

CHAPTER 24

ROBIN SAT ON the edge of her bed, her mind in turmoil. She hadn't realized how much her life was on hold because she'd never had a chance to say goodbye. She'd grieved for her parents from the moment she'd understood what had happened. It had been hard, so hard, she hadn't been able to deal with the loss of her brother at the same time. It was as if she'd compartmentalized the losses. Her parents in one and her brother in the other.

Now the last compartment had been opened. Because of Jon. The two were mixed up inside her head. Her heart. She'd never had a chance to say goodbye to Jonathon. Somehow that mattered. The shrinks would call it closure.

In theory she hadn't had the same opportunity with her parents either, but having grieved for them already, it felt like the process was complete in some way. Not so with Jonathon.

That was just stupid. How could the death of another little boy help heal the loss of the first? It couldn't. It just made two wrongs. Not one right. She flopped back on the bed, her mind dimly aware that housekeeping had come…and gone. The pungent smell of a heavy night of lovemaking was…missing. She wanted to cry. She wanted something to hang onto from last night. Something to remind herself it had been real.

Cause this was reality now. Last night was one bit of fantasy she'd hold close forever. But there was no way she'd be having a relationship with Sean. She wasn't his kind. He wasn't her kind. She didn't know what her kind was anymore, but she wasn't into one-night stands. Given that she'd done just that, he could be forgiven for thinking she was. Maybe there were people who met once a week. Met every Tuesday for servicing. His and hers kind of servicing. God, what a horrid thought.

As she lay there, a pounding on the door slowly penetrated the fog in her mind. She didn't want to see anyone. Didn't want to speak with anyone. Her mind filled in the next line automatically. Didn't want to care for anybody.

It all hurt. And she was tired of being hurt.

She froze as another truth popped into her mind. It wasn't so much that she was tired of the pain of the surgeries, but that she was tired of being hurt. Of being the one that hurt. If she didn't have more surgeries, she couldn't be hurt anymore. She wouldn't wake up in pain, live in agony for days, weeks of recovery ahead of her.

Except an innocent child had run still screaming from her – so she'd been hurt anyways. Confused, not knowing how to move forward, she'd gone inside and stayed there. She was a mess.

The truths coming at her so hard and so fast were chilling. She didn't know when the tears started. Didn't know when the door opened or when strong arms lifted her, turned her, and enclosed her against a warm hard chest.

Sean. Somehow he'd gotten into her room. She couldn't be angry. How could she be when he was all she wanted right here and now? To be held. To be loved, even if just for a moment, so that she could curl up and know someone else was there to share the burden. Even if only for a little while.

But he needed to know the truth. She really wasn't worth saving. She was small. Selfish. Weak.

In a broken voice, between the sobs, she told him. About needing to say goodbye. About needing the pain to stop. About needing to fix this now, while she could. If she could. And about not being worthy of his care…but she needed it anyways. She hoped he could stand to be with her a little longer because she didn't think she could do this alone. She didn't want to put herself to the test and fail…one more time.

She put her arms against his chest and pushed back so she could look into his face, but she could barely see as her tears flowed like a waterfall down her face. "I'm sorry," she sobbed. "So sorry."

"For what?" he whispered. "For being on this planet in the journey called life as the animal identified as a human?"

She choked, giggled, then sobbed some more.

"You can never *be* perfect. You *are* perfect. You can never be whole, you *are* whole. You can never be better than you are at this moment." He smiled so tenderly more tears welled up. "You are the best you can be right now."

She shook her head, her hair flying wildly about her head, only to end up clinging to her face. "I've done nothing. Don't you understand? I should be over this. I should have completed the surgeries by now and all this," she waved her arm at her face, "Would be over and done with. I'd look normal. Or at least as normal as I can be."

"So you can do that next week. Get back to the business of doctors and hospitals."

"Next week? Maybe." She threw up her hands. "But only if I can say goodbye this week."

There was a gentle pause.

Then he asked slowly, "What do you need to do to say goodbye?"

"I have to go to the hospital," she said painfully.

"I hate to say this, but you can't be allowed to confuse the boys – Jon is not your brother."

"No," she whispered sadly, "But you have to understand, it was *that* hospital…my brother Jonathon died there. I was in a separate hospital. I never got a chance to see him again." She stared around the room blind to her surroundings. "He died alone."

She took several shaky breaths. "The last memory I have is when we were hit. My mother screaming. My father yelling, and my brother, my baby brother, never saying a word. He just lay in a crumpled heap of broken bone and torn flesh."

"I was injured and trying to get free. Trying to get to him when the fire started. The rescue crews were trying to free us, and the flames kept growing bigger."

She stopped, her voice trembling, unable to form a word. She burrowed deeper into his chest. "I need to go to the hospital. Even if I can't see him. I need to walk the hallways. See where my brother had been. See where he'd died and if I can, say goodbye."

"How would it help to walk the hallways of the hospital that's full of children, especially since the one you want to see isn't there?"

She smiled through her tears. "I don't know that it will, but I have to try."

He stared at her intently. And he nodded.

"Let's go then."

After that, they moved quickly. After all, who knew if

they'd be allowed to see Jon and if they were, how long he actually still had.

"THANK YOU."

He stood up, wrapped an arm around her shoulder, and led her gently to the door. "Let's go. We don't have much time.

"We might not even be allowed to see him." He knew that. She'd already mentioned it once. It was as if she needed to go over everything again to reassure herself that she was doing the right thing.

He stayed silent and walked outside the hotel parking lot. He helped her into his truck and started up the engine. For someone who'd promised to never enter another hospital – especially this particular children's hospital – he was there a lot. He drove the now well-accustomed route to the hospital and parked in the visitor parking lot.

It was early afternoon now. Time they'd have normally been in the ward. They'd only been there twice, but he'd figure the third time would have been the charm for Robin. Now he realized she wasn't likely to get that third time. That was too bad.

Robin had the potential to beat a mess of issues with these kids. Jenna had been right there.

That didn't mean he liked her methodology. It had been harsh. Cruel. And incredibly terrifying for Robin. It didn't matter if she had signed up for this workshop, she hadn't known what she was signing up for.

He led the way through the hallways. It wasn't visiting hours yet, but one could get away with all kinds of things if one walked with purpose. He stopped outside the ward where they'd been for the last two days and turned back to look at Robin.

She held back. "We shouldn't disturb them."

"So what do you want to do?"

She turned back the way they'd come. "I want to find Jon."

Just then, the doors opened behind them and Andrea walked out. "Oh dear, did you not get my message?"

Sean nodded. "We did. We're so sorry to hear about him. It's Jon, isn't it?" At Andrea's nod, Sean glanced over at Robin and asked, "Is there anything we can do for him?" He nodded to the room behind them, "For them?"

Andrea shook her head. "No. At this point, we don't have an update on his condition. The kids are pretty upset. They just want some downtime."

"Is that the right thing for them?" Robin asked. "Isn't a distraction a better idea?"

"What do you suggest?" Andrea eyed Robin curiously. "Or are you just asking a general question?"

"Both in a way." Robin murmured. "I guess I won't be able to see Jon, will I?"

She shook her head. "No, he's in the ICU. No one is allowed in but immediate family."

"Does he have any?" Robin asked.

The nurse pursed her lips. "I don't actually know. Most people have someone."

Sean and Robin shared a look. "Not in our cases, we didn't," Sean said quietly. "We both understand what Jon and," he tilted his head toward the ward, "the others are going through."

Her gaze sharpened. "I hadn't known."

"No one does," Robin said. "Not really."

"Well, you might be able to stand outside Jon's room and see him, but you won't be allowed in." She turned back to the ward, and said, "As far as these guys go, I'll see how the mood is if you want to check in with me after that."

Sean smiled. Nice. "Thanks, we'll do that." He slipped an arm around Robin's shoulders and turned in the direction of the ICU unit. With any luck, she'd be able to at least see Jon from the hallway.

They walked quietly toward the ICU, Robin ever silent at his side. It took ten minutes to get where they needed to be.

With every step, the air around Robin seemed to deepen, darken.

"Are you okay?" he asked.

CHAPTER 25

"I 'M FINE," SHE whispered. "It just feels so…" She shrugged. "…odd to be here." Like it was wrong for Jon to be here.

"So do what you need to do and let's leave. We don't need to go back to the ward if you don't want to. Andrea will understand."

Robin nodded. "We'll see."

She hoped she was together enough to want to go and see the boys, but as she'd been dragging herself, kicking and screaming, to that same room the last two days…

They came into the super silence of the Intensive Care Unit.

"I wonder where he is," Robin asked, hating to look into the rooms without knowing who was on the other side. Out of the corner of her eyes, she saw movement. A mother sat down beside a bed to her left. Robin smiled. At least that person had someone who loved them.

They walked to the end where Robin stopped outside a room. She caught a glimpse of a small figure lost in the huge bed. That was Jon. She knew it. Felt it. Her instincts were screaming at her to run. That she wouldn't like what she found. That she should leave before she got too close to the issue and got hurt – again.

Run, her mind screamed. *Save yourself from more hurt,*

run.

She refused to let her feet follow those comments.

No more running for her.

She planned on staying right where she was.

For better or for worse.

She walked over to the window to see Jon's small fine-boned features looking slack and hollow-eyed. He slept, which was the best thing for him. She hated to see him lying there so alone. From outside, she had to assume it was a majorly bad turn. She could only stand and stare, her heart breaking. Was this what her brother had looked like before he'd died? Had he been all alone like Jon? The thought almost brought her to her knees.

Instantly, Sean wrapped his arm around her shoulders. "Hey, take it easy."

"He looks so lost. So alone."

"We don't know that. He's getting the best care he can get. We just have to hope." He stared into the window. "I wonder what happened."

A nurse stepped up beside him and said in a quiet voice. "There were complications from what should have been a simple surgery."

Robin gasped, her hand going to her own face. The nurse nodded. "We do our best, but sometimes, through no one's fault, things go wrong."

Robin understood the inherent truth of that statement, all the while hating the unfairness of the situation. "Is he dying?" she asked in a small voice.

"There's a chance he'll pull out of this. If he makes it through the night, he'll have a much better chance."

She hoped he made it. There was little enough she could do but whisper her prayers with all the heartfelt emotion she could put behind it. Something she hadn't had a chance to do for her brother. She wasn't religious, having been raised without, but figured there had to be someone out there to help.

She closed her eyes and bowed her head, letting a gentle prayer ripple through her thoughts. When she opened her eyes, she turned to the nurse and said, "Is there any chance I can stand beside him for moment?"

The nurse shook her head. "It's not allowed. Neither will he know that you are there."

"Just for a moment," she pleaded.

There was enough hesitation in the nurse's gaze that she pressed home the advantage. "Please, I promise I won't touch him."

Sean stepped forward. "You can go in and wait with her."

Sighing, the nurse turned and led the way over to Jon's bed. "You get five minutes. You can touch his hand but nothing else."

Robin, nervous but excited, followed. When she realized Sean wasn't following, she turned to look back at him.

He smiled reassuringly. "Go. I'll wait right here.

She gave him a brilliant smile and followed the nurse to Jon's side.

SEAN FOLLOWED ROBIN'S progress to Jon's bedside. She reached out to stroke the small hand. Then she bowed her head. He could see her lips moving. He wished he could hear what she was saying. As he watched, she talked to Jon, smiled, and maybe even laughed a little. He was amazed. What was she saying? He turned to gauge the nurse's reaction. At the softening of her features and the gentle smile on her face, he took that to mean that whatever Robin was saying was coming from heart.

And that girl had a big heart.

Watching her warmed his lonely heart. He'd never met anyone like her. Had never thought to either. Such women were for other men. Whole men.

Men who had a heart left to care.

He'd never realized he was one of them – until now.

CHAPTER 26

ROBIN WALKED OUT of Jon's room, tears in the corner of her eyes but with a smile on her face. As soon as she saw Sean, she ran to him. His arms closed lovingly around her. She nestled in close, waiting for her heart and emotions to calm down. When she could, she pulled back slightly and looked up at him. "Thanks for being here."

He dropped a kiss on the tip of her nose. "Always."

She smiled, "Now if only you meant that." She deliberately stepped out of his arms and turned to the hallway. "I'd like to go see the boys now."

His gaze narrowed. "Are you sure?"

"Yeah, I promised Jon I would." At his startled look, she added, "I don't know why…" She shrugged. "But it seemed like the right thing to say at the time."

Once there, he turned in the direction of the common room, tucked her arm into his, and led the way.

At the ward, Andrea met them at the doorway. She smiled and said, "Just for a few minutes."

The two walked a dozen feet inside and stopped. The kids turned to face them, a mixture of hope and fear on their faces. Robin smiled. "I just visited Jon. He's holding his own right now."

Andrea gasped.

The kids ran closer. "Is he getting better?" the first one

asked.

"I can't say that for sure. I can tell you that he's sleeping and the doctors are hopeful." At her words, several of the kids seemed to relax. She didn't want to give them the wrong impression, but everything she'd said so far had been the truth.

The closest boy approached. "Hi. I'm Brian."

She stiffened. It was one thing to deal with necessities. It was another when this became close and personal. Dealing with children on a one-on-one basis could get very personal. Closing her eyes briefly, and then opening them, Robin took a deep breath and whispered. "Hi Brian."

"What's wrong with your face?" he asked bluntly, in the way of children. At least they were honest. Then he added, "It looks something like Jon's. Are you dying, too?"

"No, I'm not dying," she responded lightly, knowing that the slightest negativity could send the boys into a wave of depression again. She tried to brighten her smile. "I was in an accident."

"I was in an accident, too," he said after a moment. He indicated his missing leg.

She studied his stump. He was on crutches and doing fine. "Looks like you're motoring around just fine."

He shrugged. "I'd rather have my leg back. But I'm getting a new super fast – like superhero fast – fake one. It's got weird curves in it." And he waved his arms in the air, sketching the image. She had to laugh. "So you're going to be a superhero now?"

"Nah. But maybe I'll be close." He brightened at the thought and hobbled back several paces. Several other boys joined him until a large group stood around staring at her. They were going to ask more questions. She could sense them gearing up.

Andrea stepped closer and murmured, "Are you okay?"

Robin nodded. "Sure."

She knew what the kids wanted. She couldn't hide anymore. Maybe never could. And maybe it would help them to see her as a separate person. Not related to Jon. And if they saw that she was fine and had survived all her surgeries, maybe they'd have a little more hope for Jon, too.

"Do you want to see my face?" Robin asked, proud of the calm in her voice. Better to get this over with. It would stall the questions that made them all look ready to burst.

"Yes!"

Just as she went to lift her hair back, Brian turned back to the other kids and said, "If you want to see her face, come here."

"Oh dear," Andrea said beside Robin.

She should have expected such a response. Brian seemed like a rambunctious kid and like many boys, he had a ghoulish appetite. Well, she could do that.

"Ha," she said with a real smile. "It's not even Halloween yet, maybe you guys are too scared to see."

That brought a half dozen running over.

"Now you did it," Sean said, laughing. "Nothing like showing boys something that might tweak their ghoulish senses."

"I figured better to get it over with." When all the kids were around them and she could see a few dealing with visible scars of their own, she said, "I was in a car accident many years ago. It was really bad. I'm the only one that survived."

"Did you lose your family?"

The soft voice spoke up from the left and Robin saw a

little boy she hadn't noticed before. Maybe it was because he blended into the chair so well. And had curled into a tiny ball. A protective ball. There was no visible injury, but there was no one in the room that couldn't hear the pain in his voice.

"Actually," Robin took a deep breath. "I did. I lost them all."

There were horrified and yet avid gasps from the kids.

She kept her eyes locked on the little boy now facing them. "It was really hard at the time, but now it is much easier."

The boy shrank back slightly. "I don't want it to get better," he whispered and closed his eyes.

Robin studied his tiny form and thought back to the initial days of holding on to the memories of her brother, her mother, and her father close to her. Especially when the bright memories faded, the exact words she used to remember in her mind – slipping. Then she'd hung on even harder – feeling disloyal somehow. Afraid she'd lose everything if she lost the last of them. They were her life. And now they were gone. If she couldn't keep them with her, she'd be alone.

It had taken several more months for her to realize – she was alone regardless.

"Hey, can I move your hair back?" One particularly persistent little boy asked. He had red hair standing straight up and freckles completely covering his face. Except for the long raw scar wrapped around his jaw. Swollen yet healing, it made his jaw oversized.

"I'll do it," she said. She leaned forward and said, "Ready?"

"Yes," they shouted.

She slipped a hand upward and under the long dark hair and pulled it back, leaving her face completely visible.

"Oooh."

"Wow."

"Gross."

As each of the kids ran through their favorite expressions, she couldn't help but laugh. "And now you know."

"It's not bad. Why do you try to hide it?"

"Because some people made hurtful comments, so I started hiding it." She shrugged. "Maybe I shouldn't have, but there it is."

Brian grinned. "If I had a face like that, I'd enter into a zombie movie and see if I could get a part."

She felt Sean's start of surprise at the comment. And realized he was still behind her. She dropped the hair and slid her comfort zone back into place. She turned back to the boys. "Now you guys tell me what happened to you."

Most of the kids jumped in with their war stories of accidents, surgeries, and all manner of things that could go wrong with the human body. The kids relished it. It was a chance to go over their experiences with someone who understood. Someone – an adult – who had been there.

It was a chance to be listened to. Survivor stories and a chance for their story to be the worst. The hardest. The most graphic in detail. She didn't know when she somehow ended up being one of them. When one young boy, she thought his name was Jack, mentioned the waking up in the morning with stitches and staples across his belly, she felt her insides knot.

"It's a horrible feeling, isn't it?" she said, wincing. "When you look down for that first time and you have long metal shiny things holding your insides together. That if you move the wrong way, breathe too heavy, all your guts are going to fall out."

The boys lit up at that, and the details of their experiences grew and the goriness increased. She sat back and relaxed. She'd forgotten just how accepting and non-judgmental kids really were. They didn't care if her face was scarred – they just wanted all the bloody details of how she'd gotten that way.

At least these boys did.

SEAN HAD A pencil in hand and several pieces of paper scavenged from Andrea. He'd felt the need like nothing else had felt so right in a long time. He wanted to put Robin down on paper. Preserve this part of her – in case he never saw it again. He didn't know if it was last night, Jon, the boys, a combination of all the issues, but she was looser, friendlier. Relaxed. Open. She was…special.

His hand shook with intensity as he tried to capture that look on her face. The exuberance. The liveliness. The real Robin. Or what he imagined the old Robin from before the accident was like.

He loved that the boys had taken to her. Even regaling each other with the war stories of their experiences. She'd fit right in today. The last two day's behavior was gone – as if it never existed.

Healing was like that.

He wanted to laugh and shout with joy. But he couldn't. He didn't want to draw her attention to her change in behavior. Nor take her attention away from the boys. Not when she was doing such a great job at being herself.

Of course they'd loved her face. He'd seen their mouths

twist in Os and their eyes cringe in awe and…respect.

She wore her war wounds as they did. She was older. She was an adult.

But she was one of them.

CHAPTER 27

ANDREA SAID IN a loud voice, "Okay boys, Robin and Sean have to leave. They were only here for a short visit today."

"Awww. Really?" several the boys cried out.

"We'll be back," Sean said. "Tomorrow. We'll be back for one more visit tomorrow."

"Okay."

Robin walked out backwards, waving and crying out to the boys, "Bye."

As they walked toward the elevators, she laughed and raced down the stairs, only stopping when she reached the bottom and needed to catch her breath. Sean, grinning at her side, said, "What brought that on?"

As she opened the door to the main floor, she said "I just felt an outburst of energy. Needed to move. Needed to run."

"Okay then, now that you have so much energy, what do you want to do?" Sean led the way to the exit and out to the parking lot.

"Do you know a decent restaurant around here? I'm starved."

He laughed. "I know a mean Chinese restaurant a few blocks over."

"A mean Chinese would be perfect."

He made a couple of right turns and then a left and suddenly turned into a parking lot and parked. The change was so sudden she couldn't believe that they were already here.

But she was game. And suddenly so hungry she couldn't stand it. Inside, the place was just gathering a small crowd for the dinner rush. They took a seat in the back of the large room. They were brought menus almost immediately and the waitress never had a chance to leave as they ordered immediately.

When the waitress finally left, Robin sat back with a fat smile, loving the sense of accomplishment. The sense of freedom. She'd overcome several hurdles today. She'd manage to show her scars and instead of running away from her screaming, the boys had been enthralled. She'd had the floor and they'd been a willing audience. After the emotional time with Jon, she'd been overwhelmed. Heartache had ruled. But then she realized that she had something she could do for the boys, help them feel better about Jon. She hadn't had a plan of action, but it had all happened naturally.

She was good with that.

The food arrived and she fell on it with a vengeance. Lord, it felt good to have a hot meal.

SEAN WATCHED HER eat with enjoyment. She inhaled her food. It was good to see. So was the progress she'd made. Unbelievable progress. He could only imagine where she'd be by the end of the week.

He studied her covertly. She was so focused. So appreciative. Stopping to savor the tastes in her mouth. And God, her mouth. At the tightening in his groin, he tried to focus on something else but once the floodgates had opened, memories from last night rushed through his body.

A shudder ran though him. God, he wanted her. Right here and now.

He closed his eyes and struggled for control.

"What's the matter, aren't you enjoying it?" she said in between bites. "It's good. I'm really enjoying it."

"I can tell," he said in a gritty voice and quickly polished off his plate. The sooner they left, the sooner he could get her into his bed. It was all he could think about.

She was – his mind came up blank for a moment – a butterfly, newly released from her chrysalis.

Ready to fly.

He was so glad he'd been here to see it.

As he drove back to the hotel through the heavy Vancouver traffic, he realized with a sinking feeling that she didn't need him anymore.

That she could finish this on her own.

And he'd never been more afraid. To be alone.

CHAPTER 28

THE AIR IN the truck chilled the closer they got to the hotel. She didn't really understand what was happening until they pulled into the hotel lot. She was exhausted but also seriously revved. She needed to unwind somehow. She hopped out of the truck, waited for him, then headed for her bedroom.

"Now what?" Sean asked in a cooler tone of voice than she was used to hearing. "Pool? Rest? Pub?"

Something was up. She stopped and looked at him. With a wide grin, she said, "I was thinking more along the lines of bed."

And watched as his gaze lit up and his grin turned devil-ish. "A girl after my own heart."

With a giggle she took off, leading the way to her bedroom, Sean fast on her heels.

She rolled over the next morning and grinned. Sean was sprawled on his tummy, taking up most of the room. He was a serious bed hog. He looked like he hadn't moved after collapsing in the middle of the night. It had been a night of heated sex like she hadn't known possible. Even now, her body ached all over. And she'd loved every minute of it.

She knew their time here was coming to an end, but as she stared at her hot sleeping lover, she wondered if he would be interested in trying out that whole relationship thing he said he didn't do.

Technically, two nights together was no longer a one-night stand. She knew she wanted to keep seeing him. They were dynamite in bed, and he was the only male that didn't seem to be put off by her scars. Then she hadn't given many a chance to see them.

In reality, he'd been there for her in ways she hadn't really understood. Hadn't thought such a thing was possible. She'd been wrong. As he'd shown her. She leaned over and kissed his cheek. He shifted slightly under her gentle touch. A wave of love swept over her. He'd been the catalyst for her healing this week. She wasn't done, but she was well on her way. And she had him to thank. And Jenna.

Speaking of which, she glanced over at the clock and realized she was supposed to start the morning with a one-on-one session with her. And she was going to be late. She dashed to the bathroom and her shower to get started for the day.

Even rushing, she was still late for her meeting. She stepped into the small room that Jenna had taken for business during the workshop, a take-out coffee in her hand, a big grin on her face. "Good morning. Sorry I'm late."

Jenna looked up and smiled. Her gaze seemed to see into Robin's very soul. And her smile deepened. "Looks like you had another good night."

"Well, I didn't get much sleep, but it was a great night." Robin laughed and took her seat.

"Sounds like you and Sean are getting along well."

Robin nodded. "Honestly, it's not what I expected. *He's* not what I expected, but I'm delighted with what I've learned about him."

"Good." Jenna clasped her hands together on the desk

and leaned forward slightly. "So tell me what you've learned."

That made Robin pause. Was Jenna asking what she'd learned about Sean or about herself? She wanted to ask but didn't want to go in the direction of Sean unless necessary. It seemed too personal and almost against Sean to talk about him. "This week has been tough in many ways. There's no doubt that much of my issues stem from the loss of my brother." She went on to explain the need for closure, how being able to see Jon last night had helped and how difficult going back to see the other boys afterwards had been – and how rewarding.

After she finally fell silent, there was a warm caring energy in the room.

Jenna sat back, a proud smile on her face. "That sounds like you've made wonderful strides this week."

"I have." Robin couldn't stop grinning. "And I have you and Sean to thank for that."

Immediately Jenna shook her head. "You did all the work. I provide the circumstances for the change, but you had to walk the walk."

"And I did, and I feel wonderful for having done so." She stood up. "I guess we have workshop stuff to do this morning before our last visit to the kids."

"That's right." Jenna stood up. "I'll be doing one-on-one sessions with everyone this morning, so today is really a chance to go over the report and fix anything that needs more work as well as see what other things are needed to round it out."

At the reminder of the report, Robin froze. "That's something I don't know how to help with. I have no idea what Sean has been doing on it, if anything."

"Well, it's required first thing tomorrow morning, so you have today to figure it out." Jenna's voice was firm, her face beaming as if to say 'you can do this.'

The only thing was, Robin knew she hadn't contributed anything. She hadn't even given Sean time to sketch her. And his arm hurt when he worked too long. She frowned as she wandered into the seminar. They should have gone to the hot tub last night. Let his muscles relax. She'd been letting him take care of her, but he hadn't been taking care of himself. And she, so broken up about everything going on in her psyche, had let him.

Damn. Now she felt guilty.

Inside the workshop, groups were working on their project. There was no sign of Sean. She glanced around, looking for Tania, but she wasn't here either. Out of sorts and wondering what she should do, she sat down to wait.

A half hour later, there was still no Sean. She gathered up her stuff and returned to her room. He must be still asleep. As she unlocked her door and walked back inside, she realized he wasn't asleep. Or in the shower. He was gone.

She let the door close and stood there, staring at the rumpled bed.

Maybe she should have said something to him? Woken him up? Texted him? She pulled her cell phone out of her pocket on the off chance she'd gotten a text from him, but there was none.

Making a quick decision, she walked back out, headed to his door, and knocked.

There was no answer.

SEAN SAT IN the far end of the coffee shop – the opposite

end of where he always sat with Robin. He wanted to be alone. To think. To work. To deal with his own crap. He'd already texted Paris several times, but it was hard to express what he was feeling. Then his cell phone battery had died, putting an end to the conversation. He'd forgotten to place it on his charger last night. Damn. That was something he rarely forgot.

Still, it was a good way to get out of the conversation. He wasn't used to sharing. Didn't quite know how to do it. Wasn't sure it was a good thing to be doing. He'd always kept things locked up inside. He understood the psychobabble of letting it all go, he was taking psychology classes after all, not that he'd shared that fact with many people.

He had to admit he'd learned a lot about himself while here this week. And about others. That absolute need to heal. To move on with their lives. Everyone here came from a different place on the healing scale – if there was such a thing, and everyone was approaching the problem differently. He had to wonder if Jenna was psychic with the way she'd been pairing up couples. Was that a good thing? Or was she off the marker on everyone – including him and Robin? No. In that respect, she'd been right on the money.

He brooded as he stroked and shaded his latest picture. He'd somehow amassed a large collection of sketches of Robin. He wasn't sure how or where or when, but there were some where she was a tiny image in the corner and then others where she was larger but faded. He didn't remember doing many of them, but he must have done. And he'd done four new ones already this morning.

Robin had become the biggest subject of his life. And the only one he wanted to draw. Stupid. Crazy. Paris had said so in her last text. She was probably right. He'd been called crazy more than once. His father used to call him that before slugging him across the head. Or more accurately, he'd say, "Crazy bastard."

Then beat him again. Maybe he was crazy, but it had been his way of surviving. And it had worked. But once again, he had to wonder if his mental state was something he could trust. He'd never been so lacking in certainty before. He desperately wanted a relationship with Robin. But not even he could stretch ripping up the bed sheets for some of the hottest nights of sex in his memory as a relationship.

That was a physical need. There'd been no emotional involvement in it. Except the sex had been so incredible, and he knew it was from the emotions coursing through him.

But he wasn't so sure about her.

And that was the part he was troubled about.

The last thing he wanted was for Robin to advance to a whole new world – and leave him behind. Sure, he hadn't come here for himself. And he knew this was the place for Paris. No doubt about it. But now that he could see what was available in terms of progress and healing, he wanted some of it for himself.

Just like he wanted something from the new and improved Robin – to have a place in her future.

He turned the page and started working on the next picture.

If nothing else, he'd have these images to keep his memory of her alive long after this workshop had ended.

CHAPTER 29

ROBIN FOUND HERSELF alone at lunchtime, too. She was worried about where Sean might be. Was he okay? It was almost time to leave for the hospital. She didn't know what to do. She wanted to see the kids today. Wanted to get the benefit of her last day here. She was feeling better about herself than she had in a long time. Now if only she knew what was going on with Sean? They had one more night. She was selfish enough to want it. Every last minute of it.

And she had no idea if he even cared enough to push his one-night stand rule into three nights. Had she pushed him too far already?

God, she hoped not. She dove into her meal when it arrived. The burger and fries reminded her of Sean. It was only as she finished and hopped to her feet to get ready for the hospital when she saw Sean busy working on the back corner of the room. As she walked closer, she realized that he was working on their project. She stopped and winced.

A huge load had been placed on his shoulders. She'd had to do nothing on that report. How unfair was that? She was a complete failure in the artistic department. That just made her feel worse. As she approached, maybe because she approached, he slammed his sketchbook closed and packed away his stuff. He stood up as she arrived at his table.

He stopped and stared at her, a shocked look on his face.

She frowned. "What?"

Sean frowned, looked down at his shoes briefly, then gave a half-hearted shrug. "Glad to see you. I was wondering how to track you down."

"Ah," she pulled her cell phone out of her pocket. "Cell phone." She waved it at him. "I've sent a half dozen messages, but you haven't answered any."

With a sheepish grin, he admitted, "I forgot to charge my phone last night so my phone is dead."

"Ah shit." She laughed. "I thought you were mad at me for some reason."

His eyebrows lifted. "Of course not. Why would I be mad at you?"

When he said it in such a commonsense voice, she realized that she'd been foolish. "Sorry. I wasn't thinking straight." She motioned to his sketchbook and portfolio case. "I was feeling guilty as I hadn't been able to help you."

He smiled, closed the zipper, and said, "No help required."

He pushed his chair under the table and said, "Are you ready to go to the hospital?"

She nodded. And followed him out to the parking lot.

At the hospital, they both walked the now familiar path to the children's ward. She wanted to stop in and see Jon but decided not to in case he'd taken a turn for the worse as she wouldn't be able to hide it from the kids. They could stop by afterwards. At the door, she took a deep breath and pushed it open. And walked inside.

"Robin"

"Sean."

"Hey, they're here. I told you they'd come again." Brian led the pack that was hobbling, wheeling, and limping toward them.

Robin had to admit as far as welcomes went, this one was great. She also had several things in her hands that she'd picked up this morning. Thankfully, Vancouver was a main center and almost anything could be bought right around the corner. In this case, the big mall under the city had provided a fortune in games. She'd asked Andrea what they could bring for the kids, and that had been her suggestion. Not having kids, Robin had no idea of the cost involved in buying video games. Like seriously...

The gifts were also from the both of them. She had no intention of asking Sean to pay. Not only had he had no say in what she was doing, but he was the only one doing the report that was also from her. Not to mention all the meals he'd fed her at the beginning of the week.

"What's in those bags?" Brian asked.

She laughed. "Something for you guys, but I'll show you later."

The little tiny boy sat up and looked at her. "You aren't hiding your face today."

Silence. Everyone stopped to study her new hairstyle. And she realized she'd completely forgotten about it. But it explained Sean's shock when he'd seen her earlier. She'd pulled her hair back on both sides and French-braided it down the back. The disfigured side of her face could be clearly seen.

It had felt like the right thing to do. She used to wear it that way all the time. It felt natural to do so again.

She pulled up her chair, realizing that Sean was setting up at the table like he usually did. She smiled at the little boy. "I guess I don't want to hide away anymore."

That was greeted with silence.

"It's not that bad," said the boy.

"Thank you. I'm glad you think so." And she realized that if she didn't care about who saw her face, maybe others wouldn't care either. She'd shrugged. "Besides, it's only until the next surgery…" She grinned. "Then I'll have different scars!"

The kids laughed. "Will you come back and show us?"

"Maybe I will at that. I don't have a date yet," she said, "but hopefully it will be soon."

She'd actually gone as far as calling her doctor's office and leaving a message. If she was ready to move forward, then she was ready to move all the way forward. She felt so much better, so much lighter since making that call, as if another unfinished part of her had settled into place, too.

The visit with the kids went by too fast. Before she knew it, it was time to open up the bags of gifts and hand over the new games. As the shrieks of laugher and excitement filled the air. Sean, his stuff packed up, stepped closer and murmured, "That was a great idea."

She smiled. "I wanted to make sure our parting was good for both of us."

With the kids screaming goodbyes into their ears, the two walked back out of the hospital. She looked over at Sean, who'd been so silent during the whole visit, and said, "Hey, you okay?"

He glanced over at her. "I'm fine.

She wasn't sure she believed him, but there was little she could do to get him to open up. He'd tell her if he wanted to, and only when he was ready.

VIDEO GAMES AS gifts. A great idea, and one he'd never have

thought of. Gifts were not a big part of his world. He tried to remember for Paris's sake as she'd missed so many, but it never occurred to him for anyone else. It said a lot about Robin's upbringing that she understood the appropriate times and gifts.

Trust her big heart.

"Do you want to go see Jon?"

A bright smile broke across her face. "Yes please."

Except the ICU unit was awash with people. There were different nurses on, and Jon was being attended to by several doctors.

Sean watched the worry tug on Robin's features as they stood out of the way. He waited. This had to be tough, but she'd had a chance to see Jon last night and that had been a gift. No one ever said the gift would be offered twice.

He reached over and hooked her arm to his. She cast one long look at Jon's room then resolutely turned away. He was proud of her. She'd made a lot of changes. This was yet another one.

"Let's go," she whispered.

CHAPTER 30

THEY WALKED INTO the hotel to find Jenna waiting for them. "Robin, I need to speak with you."

Surprised, her stomach sinking at the tone of Jenna's voice, Robin walked off to the side of the hallway. "I'm sorry to tell you this, but Jon, after a better prognosis this morning, has taken another turn for the worse. He's likely only got hours to live."

Robin gasped, tears welling up in to her eyes. "Oh no, I'd so hoped."

Jenna smiled, her own eyes misty. "We all did. Life is precious and it's so hard when it's taken away from us early. It's so much worse when it's a child. I'm telling you as you seemed to be so attached to him. If you still need to say goodbye…" Her voice trailed off.

Robin didn't know what to say. She'd said goodbye last night. She wouldn't be able to see him now either, especially if he was worse. As they'd just seen.

"I'm going to go to my room," she whispered. "I need some time alone." Frozen and sad, although she'd known it was a distinct possibility, she'd so hoped for a better prognosis. But why would her wishing something change anything? It hadn't helped her parents. Her brother had still died. Now Jon. Still, she had to keep hoping.

Had Sean followed her up the stairs? She was so lost in

the fog of pain and grief. She understood grief. She'd lived with it so much already. People died every day. All the time and in the most horrible of ways. She sat for a long time on the single chair by the window and stared out. What could she do? Nothing. Jon's time might end tonight, so what did she want to do? Just sit here in sadness and grief, or find a way to remember him?

She didn't want to be alone tonight. She wanted to rejoice in life. No, she wanted to celebrate Jon's life. Jonathon's life. That he'd lived and died so young was tragic, but she couldn't help it. The only thing she could do was celebrate both boys' lives. She just wished she knew how.

After washing her face, she knocked on Sean's door. He opened it, concern darkening those beautiful blue eyes. "Hey."

"Hi. Are you okay?"

She shook her head, tears forming in the corner of her eyes. "I will be, but right now I'm still…" She shrugged.

He opened his arms and she walked into them. This was what she needed. To be held. To be loved. To know that she wasn't alone. "I feel so bad for him."

"And yet it's not over. He might still pull through."

She nodded, her head rubbing up and down against his shirt. "I know that. I'm trying to stay positive."

"Do you want to go see him?"

"I don't know."

Her cell phone went off. It was Andrea.

"Robin? Apparently Jon is awake and asking for you. I hate to even call, in case this isn't something you want to do. He's not doing well."

"Oh no, Andrea," Robin said immediately. "I'll," she looked over at Sean, who was nodding, and corrected herself, "we'll be there as soon as we can."

"I'm sure he'll be happy to see you."

Without talking, Sean shrugged into his jacket and grabbed his keys.

They were at the hospital in twenty minutes. It was visiting hours this time. They walked through to the ICU and saw the same nurse they'd seen last night.

Her face lit up at the sight of them. "I'm so happy to see you. He was asking about you earlier."

Robin said in a low voice, "I understand that he's not doing well?"

"No, but the doctors are trying a new drug," she held her hands out, "I'm scared to jinx it but..." She took a deep breath and smiled. "They are cautiously optimistic. Again, he has to make it through the night. He needs strength to fight this off."

Robin walked to the doorway and looked back the nurse, who nodded. Emboldened, she walked into the small unit and sat down on the edge of Jon's bed.

He was asleep. "Jon, I'm here."

And damn it if his eyes didn't open. He tried to smile.

"You don't have to talk," Robin said. "I know you're feeling yucky."

His eyes drifted close. Then they popped open. "Did you feel this bad after your last surgery?"

She had. But it had been emotional. Psychological. Not physical. She thought about how to answer. "Not the same, but I did feel really bad."

Jon's lips curved into a tiny smile. "Good," he whispered. "I'm glad it gets better."

The words caught in her throat. "It does. You have to fight off the bad stuff and keep focused on the day when you're going to feel better."

"Do you think I'll get better?" he asked hopefully, but his gaze was dark, fearful.

"Absolutely," She remembered from her own surgeries, how important it was to stay positive. To have hope. "You have to believe it yourself. Think of good things. Happy things. Think about having ice cream with Cheerios." His eyes twinkled. "Or about kitty cats and puppy dogs."

"I love puppies," he whispered. "I always wanted one."

"Then think about the day you'll have a puppy in your arms. And think about the day you get to look into the mirror and see your face whole and great-looking. And the day you look back at your life and say it was all worthwhile."

"I can do that." Now a real smile peeped out. "I *really* want a puppy."

"And maybe when you get past this, you can have one."

They spoke for a few more minutes while he told her about the neighbor's dog that was a golden lab. As it was the first she'd heard about the neighbor or his home life at all, she stayed quiet and let him talk. After a few moments, another woman walked in. "Oh hi. Are you Robin?"

Robin nodded. She looked down at Jon and realized he'd fallen asleep.

"Thank you for coming. I know how important it was for him." She introduced herself as Cindy, Jon's mother.

Relieved to know that Jon wasn't alone, she said, "He's a wonderful little boy." Then she told her about wanting a puppy.

Cindy tried to smile, but it was interrupted by the flow of tears. "Now if we could just get him through this, I'd be happy to get him a puppy."

Sean led Robin away as Cindy sat down at Jon's bedside.

The last image Robin had was of her picking up Jon's hand and talking to him, much as Robin had.

She was sad when they walked back out of the hospital. In a soft teary voice, she said, "I'm glad he was awake."

"Hopefully he'll pull through this."

She nodded and stared up at the sky. It was overcast and dark gray. A storm moving in. "Do you want to go anywhere else or just back to the hotel?"

"To the hotel, please."

He nodded, wrapped an arm around her shoulder, and led her back to the truck.

Back at the hotel, they walked up to the elevators together. In the hallway, he stopped and looked at her. "Do you want to be alone?"

She heard the cautious note in his voice. He wanted to do the right thing. She didn't want anything to do with that.

She did not want to be alone.

"No," she whispered. "I don't. I want to forget everything negative and sad in life. I want to rejoice and celebrate life." In truth, she didn't want to be alone ever again.

He moved her toward his bedroom. "In that case," he said, a crooked smile on his face as he unlocked the door. "I think I might be able to help."

She searched his gaze, wishing he'd say something. Something to take her off this cliff of uncertainty. She'd already been blessed with the time they'd had together, but she wanted more. She'd take what she could get right now — especially if that was all there was going to be. She didn't dare do or say anything to ruin this moment. She might not get another one. "Do you think you're up to it?"

He grinned before he took her hand that rested on his chest and slid it down to the growing bulge in his pants. "I think I am. But maybe you need to make sure."

And with that, he closed the hotel door and led her to his bed.

THE NEXT MORNING, Sean was grateful to be the first one awake. Finally. He dressed quickly and slipped out to go to the coffee shop and picked up several mugs to bring back to her. When he returned, she was still asleep. He put the mugs down and kissed her awake.

She groaned.

He smiled. He could so get used to this. She opened her eyes, saw him, and smiled, a slow languid smile that set his loins to pulsing with heat again. "Unless you want to be late this morning when we have to present the report, I suggest you don't look at me that way."

"What way?" she asked, her eyes warming.

"That way, witch." He straightened and walked over to bring her the mug of coffee. "See, I've been busy already."

She propped herself up against the headboard. "I'm glad to see that." She took a sip. "Must be all that experience."

He laughed. "I don't have any of that, remember."

She smiled and took another sip.

"Besides, by my count, this is our third night together. So that's either three one-night stands in a row, which doesn't make sense," she said lightly. "Or we're in what you'd call a relationship."

He grinned. "That was my take, too."

"Except you said you didn't do those." Those intense green eyes stared at him. Was that uncertainty in her gaze? Surely not.

"I said I didn't do those." He reached over and kissed

her – hard. "Now I do." He ripped back the blankets. "And we're late. It's almost nine."

Her gaze widened. "Really? Wow, we are late."

Sean headed to the shower, wishing he could drag her in there with him, but they had no time. Drying off, he walked into the bedroom to hear her saying goodbye on her phone. "Who was that?"

"That was the hospital," she said with a brilliant smile. "Jon not only made it through the night, he's apparently doing much better this morning."

"Wow. That's great."

She bounced out of bed. "It's fantastic news." She snagged his robe off the back door, "I've got to get dressed. Do you want to wait for me or…"

"I'll be knocking on your door in ten. Then we'll need to run down to the workshop. We have to pack up and check out by noon, too."

She winced. "Crap. I'd forgotten. Okay. I'm gone."

And she bolted to her room.

Chapter 31

THEY WERE LATE. They raced into the seminar room, looking like guilty children. She was sure everyone would know. But no one said anything or even looked at them sideways. They took their seats just as Jenna saw them.

She smiled, nodded, then opened up with, "Reports are due today. I'll be addressing the teams in the back corner. When I call your name, bring your report and your partner and we'll go over them. You know the order that you fall into with one change. Robin and Sean will be last, after Tania and Kane."

The first pair stood up. And the morning started. Nerves abounded. Robin had no idea what Sean had done. She'd done her daily homework, she wasn't sure if he had, but she'd contributed nothing to the report. She wanted to say something to him about it, but he was so calm. Laid back. She envied him.

The morning passed quickly as they listened to the speakers brought in for the occasion.

Out of the blue, Jenna called out, "Tania and Kane, your turn."

Robin heard Tania's intake of breath. She turned to see her friend already standing up. The tank-like-Kane dwarfed her as they walked to the back. She wondered how their week had gone. She couldn't wait to catch up with Tania next week. It would be quite the conversation. As they weren't first, she turned to Sean and asked, "I know it's late, but is there anything I can do to help with the report?"

He smiled and said, "You already have."

"Ha. Have not."

"Have too."

She rolled her eyes and paid attention to the speakers who were visiting for the morning session while everyone gave the reports. At one point, she heard something from the back and turned around to find Tania throwing her arms around Kane, tears in her eyes.

Robin could barely hold her own back. Boy, was she looking forward to catching up with Tania.

Then it was their turn.

"Robin and Sean, please bring your report."

They both stood up. She took a deep breath. "Here we go."

At the back, there were two seats for them. They sat down, Robin now feeling horribly nervous. She'd had nothing to do with this. She didn't feel like she should be here at all.

"Sean, it's over to you."

He opened his sketchbook but held it in such a way that they still couldn't see the pages. He started speaking. "I was going to title this project Scars. After all, that's been a major part of Robin's journey, mine too. But then I realized I wanted to emphasize the positive and not the negative, so I changed it from Scars to Chrysalis."

Robin held back a strangled sound then. As he looked at her, she realized that she hadn't quite kept it back. She schooled her features and waited for him to continue.

He laid down the book and she saw the first picture was

a small sketch of her, her face small and faded on the page. There were just a few lines, but the clarity was incredible. On the same page, there were a few kids, but they were distant and unfocused on the edge of the paper. At the top of the page was a battered up caterpillar but so faint as to be a watermark.

He turned the page.

And again at the top of the page was a caterpillar, slow, swollen and heavily scarred as if it'd had a difficult life.

There her face was in greater clarity, more detailed, and so were the group of kids. She watched in awe as he moved them through several images of her and the boys, her face mostly down or hidden by her hair, and with each picture there was more detail, more clarity of her features. As if she was walking through a fog, and with each step she took her features came more into focus. In each instance, the caterpillar stayed a pale narrative of the story. So clear that even a child could understand.

Her hands clasped together as she realized how he'd taken the child aspect and run with it.

On every page, Sean narrated her journey, her self-discovery, her progress. And damn if that caterpillar watermark didn't tell the same story. At one point, it was hidden, tucked away in its cocoon. Hidden in its home…as she'd hidden in her home. The cocoon hung from a desolate branch alone and unloved…but by the very nature of the animal, Robin knew it was changing on the inside.

She listened, dazed, as he spoke of admiring her, respecting the size of the bridge she'd crossed.

He came to the second last page and was quiet for a long moment. Finally he said, "This is why I changed the name from Scars to Chrysalis."

Robin twisted around slightly so she could get a better view of the image. And gasped in shock. Her face looked like a photograph instead of a sketch and then touched up with Photoshop. She had a beautiful smile on her face, her injured side was there, but the damage somehow didn't seem to mar her features. The woman in the picture…she – glowed.

And the cocoon – the bottom had blown apart, letting the butterfly escape. And how beautiful it was. Gossamer wings, a delicate body with the hint of grace and power in its form.

Her hand to her face, she brushed the tears away. And whispered, "Oh my God, Sean, she's beautiful." She shook her head. "Both of them are."

Sean took her hand in his and said, "No, *she* isn't – no *they* aren't – *you* are beautiful." He reached up to tilt her chin and deliberately kissed her on her damaged cheek. "They are both you. And both of you are beautiful."

"How can you be so blind?" she marveled, studying the picture. And then she got it. "I thought there was a fog blocking the woman's features. But it isn't," she said excitedly. "The viewer is being led step-by-step into seeing the woman on the inside." She gazed at him, marveling at his genius. "To see the woman under the fog, under the layers."

"Or to see the woman under the…?" And he waited.

"Scars."

"I'm not blind. You are – were. Now…" He tapped the image. "Now you can see what I've seen every day. This woman emerging from behind her own self-imposed fog." He gave her a slow melting smile, and she knew she was lost forever. This man had seen her for who she truly was. And had been strong enough, brave enough to help her on her journey to see it, too.

Jenna said, from behind them. "Robin, what did you learn about Sean?"

Robin laughed, but she gazed into Sean's eyes as she spoke. "That he's a fraud. That he's been hiding in the darkness just waiting for a chance to step into the light." She shook her head and motioned toward the sketchpad. "And boy, when he stepped into the light, it was a spotlight."

She thought she'd drown in the love shining from his eyes.

"Sean?" Jenna asked. "Remember the question I asked you to answer as part of the assignment?"

Sean smiled, his gaze locked on Robin. "Turn the page."

Robin, curious, broke her gaze to watch.

The last page showed an image so powerful, so simple, with just a couple of strokes that surely it was impossible to show so much detail of the two of them. Sean held Robin in his arms, holding her as if he'd never let her go.

And there was the butterfly again, her wings fully extended, ready to take off and fly for the first time. And just above her, in darker lines, giving a more masculine defined look, was a powerful butterfly, hovering off to one side…waiting for her to take off so he could fly with her.

A sob escaped. There was a title and subtitle above the image, but Robin could barely read it for the tears coursing down her cheeks. It said,

Why Robin?

Because she's perfect…for me

Robin burst into tears and threw her arms around him.

He wrapped her up tight against his heart.

Just where she wanted to be.

Author's Note

Dear reader,

I love to hear from readers, and you can contact me at my website: www.dalemayer.com or at my Facebook author page. To be informed of new releases and special offers, sign up for my newsletter or follow me on BookBub. And if you are interested in joining Dale Mayer's Reader Group, here is the Facebook sign up page.
http://geni.us/DaleMayerFBGroup

Cheers,
Dale Mayer

Scales (of Justice)

Buy this book at your favorite vendor.

She thinks she escaped Justice

He is still waiting for Justice to happen.

She's afraid her day of reckoning is near.

He's afraid his day of reckoning will never arrive.

Will love balance the scales of Justice?

Broken and... Mending

Skin

Scars

Scales (of Justice)

Broken but... Mending 1-3

Previews

Second Chances

Go ahead. Take Charge of your life. Move forward…if you can…

Changing her future means letting go of her past. Karina heads to a weekend seminar and discovers the speaker is the person she needs to move on from. But she soon realizes bigger issues are facing her…

Brian has moved on, at least he'd believed he had… until he sees Karina in his audience…and realizes he's been lying to himself.

Passion pulls them together, love binds them together, but a revengeful enemy determines to keep the two apart…and destroy them both.

Second Chances Sample

Chapter 1

HER HEART RACING, Karina pushed open the glass double doors and walked into the almost deserted pub. Her breath quickened as she searched the faces of the few patrons inside. *Had he left already?* Or was Brian Saunders somewhere here, drowning his sorrows? Wendy, Brian's girlfriend of two years, had broken up with him and taken off for Europe, or some such thing. Karina knew she should feel sorry for him, but instead her mind wouldn't stop pestering her.

Here's your chance. One last shot to make him notice you before you go home and never see him again.

That the timing sucked wouldn't stop her.

Besides, if anyone asked, she was just here having a drink. And she could use one. Her last exam was done. She'd finally finished school and damn if she didn't feel like crying instead of cheering.

"Hey, Karina, thought you'd have booked it by now."

She waved at one of several friends having a good time at a nearby table. Most of the students who'd finished exams had already left, and the few stragglers writing tomorrow were either cramming or here trying to forget about writing in the morning.

"Nah. Leaving in the morning. It's a long drive and I *so* don't want to deal with that tonight. Or the ferry."

That elicited several nods. Anyone who lived on Vancouver Island knew about ferry woes to the mainland. She'd tossed around the idea of staying on the island, had even looked for work, but nothing had come of it, so she was heading home to Vancouver. Victoria, and the university in particular, would stay a happy memory. And, in some ways, a tough one.

She ordered a draft at the bar and turned around to take another look. Maybe she'd missed Brian in her first skim.

Shit. Ian Blackburn was here, too. And he'd seen her. Shit, shit, and triple shit. He'd always been super friendly to her, but there was something about him that gave her the creeps. And then last week she'd seen another side of him altogether. A professor in one of the classes they'd been in together had given Ian a poor grade on an assignment. Ian had lost it…big time. Someone had even called campus security to get him out of the lecture hall. He'd turned into something that terrified her and probably every other student there. She shuddered at the memory.

Karina turned around and glanced the other way, deliberately putting her back to Ian.

And there he was. *Brian.*

Her heart sighed even as it started to pound. She should go over to him. He looked sad, like he'd lost his best friend. Which, after the end of a two-year relationship, she guessed he had. But Karina told herself she was still a friend, right? Albeit a casual one, but still… They'd had classes together, the odd beer-and-pizza night as part of a group. That kind of thing. He had no idea that she'd been in love with him for a long time. She'd been careful to keep her feelings hidden. He hadn't been free and she wasn't the type to break up relationships.

She checked out the other half of the bar before her gaze zinged back to Brian. He lifted his beer bottle and poured the remaining golden liquid down his throat. Slamming the empty down, he reached for the spare, waiting. Damn, she hated to see him like this.

All right. She was going to go over there. Just a sip of beer for courage, first. She raised her glass to her lips.

"Karina. I'm glad you're here. I was hoping to see you before you left. May I sit?"

Ian. Shit. He'd somehow evaded her awareness and seated himself on the barstool next to her without her knowing. This was what she got for being nice and polite to a guy who mistook it for encouragement and, frankly, gave her the willies.

She attempted a smile behind her glass as she drowned a big gulp. She had to get away. Now.

"Sorry, I came here to meet someone." She said it lightly, dismissively. She'd planned to wait another minute or two before approaching Brian, but Ian's crowding was forcing her hand. "Oh, there he is. Brian."

She got up and waved in Brian's direction, tossing a good-bye smile at Ian.

His brows came together in a dark vee and his lips thinned, the expression causing her smile to falter and her stomach to heave. His thick nose and heavy brows might indicate a Mediterranean ancestry, but the darkness in his eyes gave her the spooks.

"I hadn't realized."

Keeping her face averted she took another big step and cast a glance back, relief washing over her when he didn't follow, but instead walked back to his seat.

Well, she'd started down this road, so…

"Hey." She slapped a bright, friendly smile on her face and sat down across from Brian. Now that she was safely seated her unease over Ian abated, even while her heart lurched at the deep unhappiness on Brian's face.

He looked up at her, a lopsided attempt at a smile peeking out. "Hi, Karina. I'm not good company right now."

"Oh." She didn't know what to say. His pain was a palpable thing. Impulsively, she reached across the table and laid her hand on his. "I heard and I'm sorry."

Surprise lit the dark depths of his chocolate eyes.

When he didn't say anything, she stood. She'd intruded on his private pain, and that wasn't right. She turned to leave.

"Wait." His husky voice reached out to her. "Please, don't go."

She smiled warmly at him and sat back down.

She stayed there for several more rounds as they talked deep into the night. Once or twice she glanced over at Ian. Every time she looked he appeared to be seething with anger as he stared toward her and Brian. She shuddered.

"This place is closing soon." She tugged Brian to his feet. "Come on, you look ready to drop."

"I'm not that bad," he protested, but allowed himself to be shuffled out the door. The cool night air hit them and snapped some of the buzz away. Karina looked at the stars, her heart full and happy. Not exactly a dream date, but it was Brian…and her…alone.

"Let's go to my place. I think I have a bottle of wine," he suggested.

"You're going to fall asleep before you ever get it open,"

she scoffed as she fell into step beside him.

He looked at her, his little-boy expression pleading that it couldn't possibly be bedtime already. "I don't want to be alone tonight," he admitted softly. "Please come share a bottle of wine with me." There was only a slight slur to his voice and she'd had just enough to drink to feel the same.

Besides, she didn't want the night to end either. It might not be the wisest move but she couldn't come up with any convincing reasons why she shouldn't spend the last few hours with him.

She gave in.

He grinned at her, wrapping an arm around her shoulders. "How come we didn't do this before?" His sloppy grin made her heart laugh. "We should have. I've always liked you."

Magical words.

They walked toward his room, arms around each other, talking, murmuring in low voices. The heat of his voice, the tenor of his words, the glow of moonlight, Brian's touch – it was magic. And she wanted more. She wanted it all. Tonight.

THE COUPLE WALKED down the path, sliding in and out of view. He'd hidden in the trees thinking to see where Brian was taking Karina. And hoping his instinctive guess was wrong.

But no; there she was. Ian thought he'd missed her leaving. But no, she'd left with Brian. Why? *Why Brian?* Brian was nothing. And he had a girlfriend. Or he'd had a girlfriend. According to the gossip, he'd just been dumped.

How could Karina do such a thing? It's not like Brian

was in any shape to enter another relationship right now. Had she no respect. For him? Or for herself?

He stood in the shadows of the trees that darkened the path and watched them make their way to Brian's dorm. Anger simmered inside.

Brian had many girls fawning all over him. He didn't need Karina. He'd only cast her off later.

Karina deserved better. If she weren't so blinded by Brian's flashy looks, she'd realize it. She'd be sorry later.

Damn Brian to hell.

SATISFACTION THRUMMED THROUGH Karina's body as she collapsed beside Brian in the wee hours of the morning. Her skin was damp and her body buzzed from their heated lovemaking. "Who'd have thought?" she whispered into the darkness.

A deep rumble rolled out from his chest as he attempted to speak but couldn't. She grinned. She'd brought him to this. She'd been the one he'd turned to tonight. Not Wendy, but her – Karina. Maybe she shouldn't have jumped at the opportunity…but she'd needed the chance to show him how good they could be together. How perfect.

And given that exams were over and all students going their separate ways, it had been now or never.

It seemed she'd loved him for so long. Always an acquaintance, never quite a friend and always superficial, kept on the outside…the last place she wanted to be.

She could no more stop blurting the words than she could stop the tidal wave of love that swept through her, giving the words their freedom.

"I love you," she whispered and dropped a kiss on his

bare chest, before nestling her head on his shoulder and falling asleep.

MORNING DAWNED BRIGHT and clear. Karina woke slowly, her body still warm and achy from the night's activities. She bolted upright as memories flooded back. *Brian.* She'd had the most wonderful night of her life. She grinned and bounded out of bed.

Wrapping herself in the sheet, she walked out to the communal room, grateful that Brian's roomies had already left. *Empty.* She stood in the middle of the room, dread forming a sinking ball of steel in her stomach. An engine started outside.

She raced over to the glass doors, stepping out onto the small verandah in time to see Brian's car disappearing down the drive at a good clip. *He was coming back, wasn't he?* She stood there, waiting, for a long time after his car disappeared from view. As her heart broke into a dozen tiny pieces, hope faded away. The small sedan was gone.

And he hadn't once looked back.

TO BE CONTINUED...

Touched by Death

Adult RS/thriller

Death had touched anthropologist Jade Hansen in Haiti once before, costing her an unborn child and perhaps her very sanity.

A year later, determined to face her own issues, she returns to Haiti with a mortuary team to recover the bodies of an American family from a mass grave. Visiting his brother after the quake, independent contractor Dane Carter puts his life on hold to help the sleepy town of Jacmel rebuild. But he finds it hard to like his brother's pregnant wife or her family. He wants to go home, until he meets Jade – and realizes what's missing in his own life. When the mortuary team begins work, it's as if malevolence has been released from the earth. Instead of laying her ghosts to rest, Jade finds herself confronting death and terror again.

And the man who unexpectedly awakens her heart – is right in the middle of it all.

This book is available. Sample chapter is next…

Touched by Death Sample

Prologue

IN PERFECT SYMPHONY the clouds swayed in the sky, wrapping the moon in protective cotton wool as the ground shook and trembled beneath the sleepy town of Jacmel in the south of Haiti.

Mother Earth growled and raged over and over again as if she knew the secrets long kept hidden in the hills behind the small town. As if she knew about the injustices done. As if she knew this had to stop. She gave one last mighty shove and the earth cracked open.

Trees toppled, their roots ripped from the ground in hapless destruction. Large rocks tumbled as their foundations were wiped out from below. Everything fell to the force of Mother Nature – at long last exposing old secrets to the light.

When she was finally satisfied, the clouds slipped back from their protective stance, letting the moon glare upon the result of Mother Earth's game of fifty-two pickup with the Devil. The rays shone on bones long picked clean – now newly exposed to the sky.

The ground undulated one last time. The surrounding hillside shuddered, sending a light dusting of earth and rock to rebury the gruesome evidence. As if the sins of man were too much for even the moon to see.

FIVE DAYS LATER, a tractor, hastily called into service, with a bucket on the front, groaned as it carried yet another load of the town's dead to a large grave. Herman, the tractor driver, was beyond pain and grief and death. He focused on the gritty details of plain survival. Five days of heat and exposure hadn't been kind to the dead – or to the living. Survival had become a grim business and rotting bodies needed to be buried or disease would crush them further. So many dead. No money. No time. No help.

No choice.

His neighbor, John, lifted the last small corpse from the dump truck load on the ground to the loader's bucket. He pulled off one work glove, straightened the bandana tied around his mouth and nose and shouted, "Good to go!"

Herman popped the gear shift forward, swore and prayed that Bertha would survive the job given her. He trundled forward. "Come on girl." He patted the stick shift in his hand. "I need you to get it done. If you quit on me, I ain't gonna make it through this." And that was no joke. He knew for damn sure that he wouldn't if ol' Bertha didn't. *Bad business this.* He had respect for the dead. Every one of his family and friends had received a proper send off, a decent burial – as was fitting. Until this earthquake.

Pain clutched his heart and squeezed. So many dead.

He'd lost his wife, one son and two grandkids this last week. Sex and age hadn't mattered here. Mother Nature hadn't cared. She'd wiped them all out.

John, the only other person who'd stepped up to help, had been lucky. His young wife and her family had survived the devastation. Living out of town had helped. That also contributed to his motivation to help out. This grave butted against his wife's family's land so it made sense for John to make sure this grave was closed over right and proper. There could be many people trekking to the grave on All Soul's Day, as families came to honor their dead. Then again, complete families had been buried together. There might not be anyone left to mourn.

He would come and visit. There were too many people here to forget.

Herman tugged at the old t-shirt tied around his nose and mouth, his black skin blending with the poor light. Nothing kept the smell out. He'd already gone through a half dozen pairs of gloves. But without the makeshift bandana the breath caught in his chest, making him gag. His clothes would have to be burned after this. There would be no way to clean them.

Bertha struggled forward. Darkness hid the evidence of what they were doing. What he'd done. He only hoped he wouldn't have too many more loads to haul.

In the aftermath of the earthquake, everyone had been numb, in shock or frozen with grief. No one had been able to make decisions. There'd been no army to take care of the problem. The government buildings and staff had been as decimated as the rest of the population.

Herman hadn't been able to leave his people lying exposed like that. Determined to do what he could he'd taken command and had done something. Something so awful, he couldn't close his eyes without seeing the stares of the dead – blaming him.

So far, close to sixty people had gone into this pit. The natural depression, a ready-made burial spot, was a godsend to the desperate survivors, a fast answer to the bloated dead rotting on the sidewalks. He didn't know how many more were to come, maybe hundreds. Later, much later, if someone cared, they could open this mass grave and do the right thing. But not now. Now they had to get on with the business of survival.

Mother Nature was a bitch.

Chapter 1

One year later…

JADE HANSEN TWISTED in the cool sheets. Her sweaty panicked body searched for a way out of the endless nightmare of bloated bodies, desperate people and cries for help – pleas that would never get answered. She turned in the fog as one more person, caught among the fallen rocks, cried out to her. She came face to face with a woman – blood congealed in her hair and streaked down the side of her face, a chunk of concrete crushing her legs. She begged for Jade to find her son.

Screaming, Jade took off to the safety of the tent, the tent filled with the dead…and the living that searched for their families.

She couldn't help them all.

She couldn't help any of them.

She couldn't even help herself.

With tears streaming down her face, Jade woke in a panic as if the demons of her nightmare had followed her into the present.

Shuddering, she recognized the hanging lamp overhead as the one in her apartment. The Aztec print couch she'd fallen asleep on was hers, a gift from her brother. And she finally understood that the evening's in-depth television coverage of a small earthquake in Haiti had been the trigger for her nightmare.

Jade curled into a ball, pulling her throw higher up on her neck. She winced at the images still flashing on the news. Another earthquake in Haiti. Only a little one this time. Not that the size mattered. The memories of her one and only humanitarian trip to that area, after the major earthquake almost a year ago, had etched themselves permanently into her brain. A horrible time, a-praying-on-your-knees-for-help kind of horrible time. In Haiti, nightmares had destroyed her sleep. The shortage of food for those suffering had destroyed her appetite.

She'd lost weight over there, but nothing compared to the pounds that had slipped off after her return home. Sure, that had been almost a year ago. It didn't matter. With the nightmare fresh in her mind it felt like only two days.

So much pain and suffering. *So much torment.* She couldn't stop it. She couldn't even begin to make it right. There'd been nothing she could do to help – or so little relative to the scope of the problem, it might as well have been nothing. If she'd been offered a ride out of that hell on any given day, she'd have jumped over her colleagues to grab it.

She wasn't proud of that.

In fact, it made her feel small and ashamed. Her colleagues had done so much better.

She'd wanted to be better. She'd tried to be better.

She'd failed. Failed her colleagues. The victims. And herself.

The memories still haunted her.

She had her nice safe lab job back in Seattle. She drove to work every day in a nice car and returned home every night to her clean safe apartment with running water, heat and electricity. All the comforts denied the Haitians still struggling through the devastation.

After she'd locked her front door behind her that first day home, the tears had started to pour. It seemed she'd been crying ever since.

Her life had gone from bad to worse for a while before she'd picked up – somewhat.

And now another earthquake.

If a small one like that triggered her memories what was the reality doing to all those poor people still living the horror?

The phone rang.

She ignored it.

It wouldn't quit. Finally, she couldn't stand it so picked up the receiver. She didn't even bother to check the caller ID. Duncan called every night at nine.

"I'm fine, Duncan."

"Hey, Kitten." Her brother's pet name for her made her smile as he'd probably intended. She used to be like him. Upbeat, funny and carefree. Until life had dumped her on her ass at the top of the slide and given her a hard kick downhill. She wasn't sure she'd hit bottom now either.

"I've got a job proposition for you."

His cheerful voice made her want to smile. The job proposition didn't. "I don't want to hear it."

He laughed, a buoyant sound that rang around the room. He never failed to raise her spirits. The effect just didn't hang around after his calls. "Maybe you don't, but maybe you do. How will you know if you don't hear it? It's a good one."

His wheedling tone made her smile in spite of her horrible mood. "Not if I don't want to hear it."

"You don't know what you want."

Jade groaned. "If I don't know, then how do you?"

That laughter pealed again. She shook her head and felt the lightness – the joyful spirit that was her brother – ease the ache in her soul. "I know you keep trying to save me, Duncan, but I'm fine."

The laughter and joy cut off suddenly. Duncan's voice, sober and sad, whispered, "No. No, you're not."

Tears choked her. She rubbed her eyes. She wasn't going to cry, damn it. Not tonight. Not *again* tonight.

"This has to stop, Jade. You're going to collapse and I don't want that to happen." Love slipped through the phone receiver making it harder to hold back the tears. Jade didn't trust herself to speak. She sniffled ever so slightly.

"I know you're hurting inside. I feel it and I hurt for you."

"I know," she whispered, starting to shake, knowing she had to stop – only she didn't know how. And once again – couldn't deal with it. "Look, I'm really tired. I need to get to bed. I'll talk to you tomorrow."

She didn't give him a chance to say good-bye and hung up instead. As soon as the receiver clicked down, the tears rolled. Hot and steady, they streamed down her cheeks. She snuggled back into the couch and let them run.

The point of stopping them was long gone – besides she no longer knew how.

"HEY DANE. THAT guy called again." John called out.

"Yeah, which guy?" Dane walked over to stand beside his stepbrother who'd stopped by the site for a visit.

Dane tugged his hard hat off to wipe the sweat running

down his forehead. Christ it was hot and humid here. He surveyed the hospital construction site in front of them. Not bad at all. They were ahead of schedule, but completion of the new wing was still months away. Jacmel hadn't recovered from the last big earthquake and with smaller ones continually causing setbacks, the country would be years getting back on its feet.

It had taken weeks to convince John to let him come over after the quake. When he'd realized how badly in need the town was, Dane had stepped in. But John had refused Dane's help to fix John's small engine repair shop that had been decimated in one of the smaller more recent earthquakes. John said he wanted to fix things himself.

"The guy about the grave." John said, "Remember they want to open it and retrieve some guy's family?"

Dane glanced over at his brother. There were only the two of them left in the family. Both stubborn. Independent. And family oriented. It had only taken one phone call with something odd in John's voice to catch Dane's attention. He'd put his Seattle construction business in the hands of his capable foreman, an old school friend, and without his brother's invite, he'd flown to Haiti two days later. That had been months ago.

Shielding his eyes from the hot sun, Dane said, "I have to admit, never-ending sunshine and warm, dry weather is hardly a hardship. Of course we haven't hit the humid summer season, yet."

"See? Isn't this much better than the wet misery of the coast? Seattle is probably still buried in snow – even in March." John grinned with satisfaction.

Dane couldn't argue that. His foreman had been complaining of just that in the last phone call. "Not everyone hates the rain like you do."

"Come on, admit it." John reached over and smacked Dane's shoulder. A cloud of dust rose, making him step back hurriedly. "You love it here."

"I love visiting you and of course, I adore Tasha." Dane grinned over his white lie. There was no arguing that Tasha obviously adored his brother so that was good enough for him. It had, after all, been the call of family that had brought Dane here.

John had a terrible history with relationships. His long-time high school sweetheart had walked out the door of her home one day just weeks before graduation and had never returned. A few years later, John had married the witchy Elise. That marriage had been a walking disaster right from the wedding reception. Dane hadn't been able to stand the woman and the feeling had been mutual. John was just a big teddy bear who attracted unscrupulous people.

After that fiasco, John disappeared for years before finally setting up housekeeping with Tasha in Haiti. Dane's antennae went off at that and given the past, he could be forgiven for worrying about his brother. Only John appeared to have stabilized, was flourishing even. Dane had been delighted.

The major earthquake had changed all that, sending John back into the same morose angry man as before.

"Hey, are you in there?"

Dane started.

John smirked at him, a sign his light-hearted kid brother was showing through the more cynical angry one of recent years. "What's the matter; Felice getting to you?"

Heat washed over Dane's throat. Felice was too hot, too willing and way too young. She was also the daughter of one of Tasha's friends who'd visited yesterday. He didn't know the specific laws in Haiti relating to that sort of thing, still he was pretty damn sure he'd get jail time back home and that was deterrent enough for him.

"She needs to be locked away for a few years."

"Not here. Girls her age are often married and pregnant." John added thoughtfully, "And not likely in that order."

Dane shook his head. "As long as it's not to me."

John changed the subject abruptly. "What am I going to do about the call...about this guy's request for help at the mass gravesite? Sounds crazy to me."

Easily following the lightning shift of his brother's mind, Dane said, "What's to do – he's a grieving man. His request isn't unreasonable. And it's done all the time."

John visibly shuddered. "I never expected to feel so strongly about it, but after that earthquake... I don't know Dane. I saw too much death. More than I should have – more than anyone should have. It seems wrong to dig up those poor earthquake victims again."

"You've been living here too long. Some weird Haitian's beliefs are rubbing off on you."

John snickered, making Dane laugh. "Or not long enough. According to Tasha, Mother Earth claimed them and she won't be happy if she's forced to give them up again."

With a sigh of disgust, Dane said, "That's crazy talk. This guy lost his family. He wants to take the three of them home to Seattle and bury them properly. He needs closure. That's all. What's so wrong about that?"

John kicked a stray rock in the dirt. "I don't know that anything is wrong with it. I guess if it were me and mine, I'd want to take them home, too. But it's a mass grave. There are other bodies to consider. Other families who will be hurt."

"Really?" Dane stared at him. "Like *how mass?*"

John shot him a look before grimacing and staring off in the horizon. "I stopped counting at sixty. We did what we had to do. The dead…they were everywhere. Herman, our old neighbor, used his loader…Christ it was bad."

Dane scrunched his face. John rushed to explain.

"God, there were children playing beside bloated bodies. They'd become dulled to them; there were so many. Oh don't blame the children. They stayed close to the people they knew because they had no one else. That a dead mother or sibling lay within a few feet didn't seem to matter. Even dead, they were a comfort."

Dane closed his eyes as terrible images flooded his mind. He couldn't imagine the horror. "I wasn't judging. I just can't envision what you went through. And to think of children sitting there, so lost and alone… Well…it's a terrible thought."

Shadows darkened John's eyes. Dane was sorry for what John had been through. "That's the thing about family." Dane patted John on the shoulder and noticed his brother cringe.

"So you think this guy should be allowed to come in and remove his kin?" John wasn't backing away from this one.

"I don't have any say in this. I wasn't aware that you did, either. I'm sure this man has already gone through the authorities. I'd suggest that you accept that this is going to happen whether you want it to or not. The team of specialists is going to be here soon. When they arrive, be nice to them. Helpful. They will probably be there for a day or two, a week or two max. Then they'll be gone, leaving the others to rest in peace."

"It's not that easy."

"I know. There are other people with loved ones in that grave. Maybe someone should suggest that all the victims be identified and even…" Dane pursed his lips and nodded his head, pleased with his idea. "Reburied properly. This guy has money. Maybe some of it should be put toward assisting the community to help them deal with disaster."

John shook his head. "You don't understand the full scope of the problem here. There could be hundreds of bodies there. We just kept putting them in then piling dirt and rocks on top to make sure they weren't disturbed. We probably went overboard on that part."

Dane blanched. "Hundreds?" He swallowed heavily. "Okay so maybe the team will need a little longer. Still something could be done for the other remains." Dane winced. "Or at least the remains they can find and identify while they search for the ones they are shipping back to Seattle."

John stared at him, and gulped. "That's not helping."

"Yeah. I know. Sorry about that."

The two men stared at the half-completed building in front of them. Dane took an involuntary step back. Right now the damn thing resembled a skeleton reaching out of the ground.

TO BE CONTINUED…

Tuesday's Child

What she doesn't want…is exactly what he needs.

Shunned and ridiculed all her life for something she can't control, Samantha Blair hides her psychic abilities and lives on the fringes of society. Against her will, however, she's tapped into a killer – or rather, his victims. Each woman's murder, blow-by-blow, ravages her mind until their death releases her back to her body. Sam knows she must go to the authorities, but will the rugged, no-nonsense detective in charge of tracking down the killer believe her?

Detective Brandt Sutherland only trusts hard evidence, yet Sam's visions offer clues he needs to catch a killer. The more he learns about her incredible abilities, however, the clearer it becomes that Sam's visions have put her in the killer's line of fire. Now Brandt must save her from something he cannot see or understand…and risk losing his heart in the process.

As danger and desire collide, passion raises the stakes in a game Sam and Brandt don't dare lose.

Broken Protocols

Romantic comedy & suspense

Dani's been through a year of hell...

Just as it's getting better, she's tossed forward through time with her orange Persian cat, Charmin Marvin, clutched in her arms. They're dropped into a few centuries into the future. There's nothing she can do to stop it, and it's impossible to go back.

And then it gets worse...

A year of government regulation is easing, and Levi Blackburn is feeling back in control. If he can keep his reckless brother in check, everything will be perfect. But while he's been protecting Milo from the government, Milo's been busy working on a present for him...

The present is Dani, only she comes with a snarky cat who suddenly starts talking...and doesn't know when to shut up.

In an age where breaking protocols have severe consequences, things go wrong, putting them all in danger...

It's a Dog's Life

Romantic comedy & suspense

It's the first day of Ninna's job in the local animal shelter...and a dog is talking to her. Not just any dog...a fat, old, smart-alecky Basset Hound who says his name is Mosey.

She can't quit, she needs this job. And then there's the yummy vet. Who turns out to live across the street from her in a much bigger house than her tiny house. Big enough to hold a few animals – including the mouthy Mosey. With all this going on, she doesn't have time to worry about the rash of break-ins and the sense of being watched. She's too busy worrying that she's nuts.

When Ninna agrees to dog sit for the cute vet from work, she sees it as a trial at being a pet owner and a way to build on her budding relationship with the vet. For Mosey, this weekend means time to get to know each other.

For the stalker who's tracking Ninna's movements, it means...opportunity.

About the Author

Dale Mayer is a *USA Today* best-selling author, best known for her SEALs military romances, her Psychic Visions series, and her Lovely Lethal Garden cozy series. Her contemporary romances are raw and full of passion and emotion (Broken But … Mending, Hathaway House series). Her thrillers will keep you guessing (Kate Morgan, By Death series), and her romantic comedies will keep you giggling (*It's a Dog's Life*, a stand-alone novella; and the Broken Protocols series, starring Charming Marvin, the cat).

Dale honors the stories that come to her—and some of them are crazy, break all the rules and cross multiple genres!

To go with her fiction, she also writes nonfiction in many different fields, with books available on résumé writing, companion gardening, and the US mortgage system. All her books are available in print and ebook format.

Connect with Dale Mayer Online

Dale's Website – www.dalemayer.com
Twitter – @DaleMayer
Facebook Page – geni.us/DaleMayerFBFanPage
Facebook Group – geni.us/DaleMayerFBGroup
BookBub – geni.us/DaleMayerBookbub
Instagram – geni.us/DaleMayerInstagram
Goodreads – geni.us/DaleMayerGoodreads
Newsletter – geni.us/DaleNews

Also by Dale Mayer

Published Adult Books:

Psychic Vision Series

Tuesday's Child

Hide'n Go Seek

Maddy's Floor

Garden of Sorrow

Knock, Knock…

Rare Find

Eyes to the Soul

Now You See Her

Shattered

Into the Abyss

Psychic Visions Books 1–3

Psychic Visions Books 4–6

Psychic Visions Books 7–9

By Death Series

Touched by Death – Part 1

Touched by Death – Part 2

Touched by Death – Parts 1&2

Haunted by Death

Chilled by Death

By Death Books 1–3

Second Chances...at Love Series
Second Chances – Part 1
Second Chances – Part 2
Second Chances – complete book (Parts 1 & 2)

Charmin Marvin Romantic Comedy Series
Broken Protocols
Broken Protocols 2
Broken Protocols 3
Broken Protocols 3.5
Broken Protocols 1-3

Broken and... Mending
Skin
Scars
Scales (of Justice)
Broken but... Mending 1-3

Glory
Genesis
Tori
Celeste
Glory Trilogy

Biker Blues
Biker Blues: Morgan, Part 1
Biker Blues: Morgan, Part 2
Biker Blues: Morgan, Part 3

Biker Baby Blues: Morgan, Part 4

Biker Blues: Morgan, Full Set

Biker Blues: Salvation, Part 1

Biker Blues: Salvation, Part 2

Biker Blues: Salvation, Part 3

Biker Blues: Salvation, Full Set

SEALs of Honor

Mason: SEALs of Honor, Book 1

Hawk: SEALs of Honor, Book 2

Dane: SEALs of Honor, Book 3

Swede: SEALs of Honor, Book 4

Shadow: SEALs of Honor, Book 5

Cooper: SEALs of Honor, Book 6

Markus: SEALs of Honor, Book 7

Evan: SEALs of Honor, Book 8

Mason's Wish: SEALs of Honor, Book 9

SEALs of Honor, Books 1–3

SEALs of Honor, Books 4–6

Collections

Dare to Be You...

Dare to Love...

Dare to be Strong...

RomanceX3

Standalone Novellas

It's a Dog's Life

Riana's Revenge

Published Young Adult Books:

Family Blood Ties Series

Vampire in Denial

Vampire in Distress

Vampire in Design

Vampire in Deceit

Vampire in Defiance

Vampire in Conflict

Vampire in Chaos

Vampire in Crisis

Vampire in Control

Vampire in Charge

Family Blood Ties Set 1–3

Family Blood Ties Set 1–5

Family Blood Ties Set 4–6

Family Blood Ties Set 7–9

Sian's Solution – A Family Blood Ties Short Story

Design series

Dangerous Designs

Deadly Designs

Darkest Designs

Design Series Trilogy

Standalone

In Cassie's Corner

Gem Stone (a Gemma Stone Mystery)

Time Thieves

Published Non-Fiction Books:

Career Essentials

Career Essentials: The Résumé

Career Essentials: The Cover Letter

Career Essentials: The Interview

Career Essentials: 3 in 1